It Was Too Late To Think Rationally As Cole's Lips Brushed Hers.

No pressure, no demand, just…touching.

As the kiss slowly deepened, Marty felt as if she'd been asleep for a hundred years and had woken up in a brand-new world to the tantalizing scent of soap and leather and sun-warmed male skin, to the iron-hard arms that held her breathlessly close.

Her carpenter. Her kissing carpenter, her upstairs man.

"Well," she breathed, unable to think of anything else to say. "Well…"

"I guess we got that out of the way," Cole said, sounding a tad stunned himself. "You want to fire me? I'll understand."

Marty shook her head. Fire him? Things might be infinitely more complicated after this, but if she let Cole walk away, she might lose the opportunity of a lifetime.

Dear Reader,

It's Valentine's Day, time for an evening to remember.
Perhaps your perfect night consists of candlelight and a special
meal, or a walk along a deserted beach in the moonlight, or a
wonderful cuddle beside a fire. My fantasy of what the perfect
night entails includes 1) a *very* sexy television actor who starred
in a recently canceled WB series 2) a dark, quiet corner in an
elegant restaurant 3) a conversation that ends with a daring
proposition to… Sorry, some things a girl just has to keep a
secret! Whatever your evening to remember entails, here's
hoping it's unforgettable.

This month in Silhouette Desire, we also offer you *reads* to
remember long into the evening. Kathie DeNosky's *A Rare
Sensation* is the second title in DYNASTIES: THE ASHTONS,
our compelling continuity set in Napa Valley. Dixie Browning
continues her fabulous DIVAS WHO DISH miniseries with
Her Man Upstairs.

We also have the wonderful Emilie Rose whose *Breathless
Passion* will leave you…breathless. In *Out of Uniform*,
Amy J. Fetzer presents a wonderful military hero you'll be
dreaming about. Margaret Allison is back with an alpha male
who has *A Single Demand* for this Cinderella heroine. And
welcome Heidi Betts to the Desire lineup with her scintillating
surrogacy story, *Bought by a Millionaire*.

Here's to a memorable Valentine's Day…however you choose
to enjoy it!

Happy reading,

Melissa Jeglinski

Melissa Jeglinski
Senior Editor
Silhouette Books

Please address questions and book requests to:
Silhouette Reader Service
U.S.: 3010 Walden Ave., P.O. Box 1325, Buffalo, NY 14269
Canadian: P.O. Box 609, Fort Erie, Ont. L2A 5X3

DIXIE BROWNING

Her Man Upstairs

Silhouette®

Desire

Published by Silhouette Books

America's Publisher of Contemporary Romance

SILHOUETTE BOOKS

ISBN 0-373-76634-3

HER MAN UPSTAIRS

Visit Silhouette Books at www.eHarlequin.com

Printed in U.S.A.

DIXIE BROWNING

has won numerous awards for both her paintings and her romances. A former newspaper columnist, she has written more than one hundred category romances. Browing is a native of North Carolina's Outer Banks, an area that continues to provide endless inspiration.

One

Marty allowed herself ten minutes, start to finish, to shower, shampoo the stink out of her hair, dress and get back downstairs in time to meet the fourth carpenter. *If* he even bothered to show up. What the devil had happened to the work ethic in this country?

She knew what had happened to her own. It fluctuated wildly between gotta-do, gonna-do and can't-do. Between full speed ahead and all engines reverse, depending on the time of the month.

At least she had no one depending on her for support. Not even a cat or a dog, although she was thinking about getting one. Something to talk to, something to keep her feet warm in bed at night while she read herself to sleep. But then there were all those shots and flea medicines and retractable leashes and collars and tons of kibble.

So maybe a couple of goldfish...?

She checked her image in the steam-clouded bathroom mirror, searching for signs of advancing age. "At least you're not paying rent. Except for the phone bill, the power bill and property taxes, you don't owe a penny to anyone."

On the other hand, her split ends were in desperate need of a trim and the sweater she was wearing dated back to her junior year in college. Even if she could've afforded to update her hairstyle and her wardrobe, she lacked the interest, and *that*—the lack of interest—was the scariest of all. She was sliding downhill toward the big four-oh, which meant that any day now, the guarantees on various body parts would start running out. Oh sure, her teeth were still sound, and she could still get by with drugstore reading glasses, but she plucked an average of three gray hairs a day; she was collecting a few of what were euphemistically called "laugh lines"; and lately her back had been giving her trouble.

Of course, moving a ton and a half of books and bookshelves single-handedly might have had something to do with that.

Bottom line, she wasn't getting any younger. Her income was zilch minus inflation, her savings account had earned the lofty sum of a buck eighty-seven in interest last month, and with the least bit of encouragement she could become seriously depressed. She read all those magazine articles designed to scare women and sell pharmaceutical products. The trouble was, scare tactics worked.

Frowning down at her Timex, Marty decided she'd give him ten more minutes. Traffic jams happened, even in Muddy Landing, population just shy of a thousand. She'd forgotten to ask where he was staying, when he'd called late yesterday to see if she still needed a builder. If he was coming from Elizabeth City and happened to get behind a tractor or a school bus, all bets were off.

Squeezing the moisture from her thick chestnut-colored hair, she tried to hedge against disappointment by telling herself that he probably wouldn't show at all, and even if he did, he probably wouldn't be able to fit her into his schedule anytime soon. If he did manage to fit her in, she probably couldn't afford him. But the biggie was her deadline. If he couldn't meet that, then there'd be no point in even starting.

"Well, shoot," she whispered. When it came to looking on the bright side, she was her own worst enemy. So what else was new?

The first time the idea had occurred to her, she'd thought it was brilliant, but the longer it was taking to put her plan into action, the more doubts were seeping in.

Was that a car door slamming?

She gave her hair a last hurried squeeze with the towel and then felt in the top drawer with one hand for a pair of socks. Having long since gotten out of the habit of matching her socks and rolling them together, she came up with a short and a long in two different colors. Tossing them back, she raced for the stairway, bare feet thudding on the hardwood floors.

At least she no longer reeked of polyurethane. If the cinnamon had done the trick, neither would her house.

The phone rang just as she hit the third step down from the top. Swearing under her breath, she wheeled and raced back to catch it in case it was her carpenter asking for instructions on how to find her address.

"Hello! Where are you?"

"Is he there yet?"

Her shoulders drooped. "Oh, Sasha." If there was an inconvenient time to call or drop by, her best friend would find it. From anyone else Marty might think it was a power thing. "I thought you were someone else. Look, I don't have time to talk now. Can I call you back?"

"You're talking, aren't you?"

"But I'm in a hurry—so can it wait?"

"Is he there yet?"

"Is who there—here?"

"Your carpenter, silly! Faylene said Bob Ed said he was going to call you yesterday. Didn't he even call?"

Marty took a deep breath, drawing on the lessons of a lifetime. Patience was a virtue, right up there with godliness and cleanliness. At various times, she'd flunked all three. "Somebody's here, I just heard a car door slam. It might be him—he. Listen, later I want to know exactly what you two have been up to, but not now, okay?"

If you couldn't trust your best friend, whom could you trust?

"Wait, don't hang up! Call me as soon as he leaves, okay? Faylene said—"

Marty didn't wait to hear what Faylene had said. The trouble with a small town like Muddy Landing was that aside from fishing, hunting and farming, the chief industry was gossip. By now probably half the town knew what she planned on doing to her house, who was helping her do it, and how much it was likely to cost her.

Slamming the phone down, she peered through the front bedroom window to see a ratty looking pickup with a toolbox in back and a rod-holder on the front bumper, a description that fit roughly half the vehicles in Muddy Landing. There was probably a gun rack in the back window, too, and an in-your-face sticker peeling off the back bumper.

Well, so what? If the guy could read a blueprint and follow simple instructions, she didn't care what his politics were or what he drove or what he did in his spare time.

Not that her drawings bore much resemblance to blueprints, but at least she'd indicated clearly what she wanted done. Not only indicated, but illustrated. If he could read, he should be able to do the job. If it weren't for all the red tape involved with permitting and such, she could probably have done it herself, given enough time. There were how-to books for everything.

She watched from the window as a long, denim-covered leg emerged from the cab. Putty-colored deck shoes, Ragg socks, followed by leather clad shoulders roughly the width of an ax handle. Judging by all that shaggy, sun-streaked hair, he was either a surf bum or he'd spent the summer crawling around on somebody's roof nailing on shingles. All up and down the Outer Banks, building crews were nailing together those humongous McMansions on every scrap of land that wasn't owned by some branch or another of the federal government. She'd like to think of all the tourists who would pour down here once the season got underway as potential customers. Trouble was, there were enough bookstores on the beach so that few, if any, tourists were likely to drive all the way to Muddy Landing, which wasn't on the way to anywhere.

She was still watching when her visitor turned and looked directly at the upstairs front window. Oh, my…

As she flicked the curtains shut, it occurred to Marty that living alone as she did, inviting all these strange men into her home might not be the smartest thing. This one, for instance, looked physically capable of taking out a few walls without the aid of tools. *He's a construction worker, silly!* she told herself. *What did you expect, a ninety-seven-pound wimp?*

She was halfway down the stairs when the doorbell chimed—three steps farther when the smoke alarm went off with an ear-splitting shriek. "Not now, dammit!"

She galloped the rest of the way and reached the bottom just as the front door burst open.

"Get out, I'll take care of it!" a man barked. He waved her toward the open front door.

Swinging around the newel post, Marty collided with him in the kitchen doorway. She stood stock-still and stared at the billowing smoke that was rapidly filling the room.

"Try not to breathe! Where's your fire extinguisher?"

"Beside the drier!" Marty yelled back. Racing across the room, she jumped and slammed her fist against the white plastic smoke detector mounted over the utility room door. The cover popped off, the batteries fell out and the ear-splitting noise ceased abruptly.

In the sudden deafening silence they stared at each other, Marty and the stranger with the shaggy, sun-bleached hair and the piercing eyes. The stranger broke away first, wheeling toward the range where clouds of pungent smoke rose toward the ceiling.

"Get out of my way!" Marty shouldered him aside and grabbed the blackened pie pan with her bare hand. Shoving open the back door, she flung it outside, took two deep breaths and hurried to turn off the burner.

The stranger hadn't said a word.

Trying not to inhale, she clutched her right hand and muttered a string of semi-profane euphemisms. God, she could have burned her house down!

"You want to tell me what's going on here?" Fists planted on his hips, the stranger stared at her warily.

He wanted answers from *her*? She wasn't the one who'd burst into a house uninvited and started shouting orders. At least he wasn't wearing a ski mask over his face and carrying an AK-whatchamacallit—one of those really nasty guns.

Of course, she'd been expecting a carpenter. And he did have a toolbox in the back of his truck. But for all she knew, the thing could be full of nasty weapons of mass destruction.

A big fan of hard-edged suspense, Marty often let her imagination get the better of her. Not only that, but she'd been under a growing amount of stress, which always tended to affect her common sense.

"Sorry about that," he said quietly, pulling her back to reality. "I thought you had a real fire going." He waved away the pungent fumes with one hand.

Trying not to breathe too deeply, she leaned over the sink and held her stinging fingers under cold running water. Ow-wow-ee!

She felt him right behind her and tried not to react. He *had* to be her carpenter—either that or a fireman who just happened to be passing by 1404 Sugar Lane and smelled smoke.

Or the answer to a harried maiden's dream?

Not that she was a maiden. Far from it.

Way to go, Owens—so much for getting your head together. You nearly burn down your house and now you're checking out the vital statistics of the first man on the scene.

"Uh—maybe I'd better leave, okay?" The voice was rich and gravelly, if somewhat tentative. Pavarotti with a frog in his throat.

"No! I mean, please—I need you. That is, if you're the carpenter I was expecting. You are...aren't you?" She turned, still clutching her wrist to keep the pain of her burned fingers from shooting up her arm.

He was staring, probably trying to decide if it was safe to hang around. "Ma'am, are you sure you're all right?"

He'd called her "ma'am." Pathetically un-PC, but sweet, all the same. Conscious of her dripping hair and her naked feet, Marty tried to look cool and in control of the situation. *Oh, Lord, did I remember to fasten the front of my jeans?*

In case she hadn't, she tugged her sweater down over her hips. A smile was called for, and she did her best, which probably wasn't very convincing. At least, her would-be rescuer didn't look convinced. Any minute now he'd be calling for the butterfly squad.

Deep breath, Owens. Get it in gear. "Sorry. I'm usually not this disorganized." At least, this time of day she wasn't. Early mornings were another matter. She was a zombie until she had her fix of caffeine and sunshine. "It's just that everything happened at once. First the phone, then the doorbell, then the smoke alarm."

He nodded slowly. Then he sniffed, using a really nice nose. Not too big, not too straight—just enough character to keep the rest of his features from looking too perfect. "What *is* that smell?"

Marty sniffed, too. The air was rank. "Polyurethane and paint thinner, uh, laced with fried cinnamon. Actually, not all my ideas work out the way they're supposed to. You ever have one of those days when everything goes cronksided?"

He continued to watch her as if he suspected her of being a mutant life-form. His eyes, she noted, were the exact color of tarnished brass. Sort of greenish blue, with undertones of gold. Looking uneasy, he was backing toward the front hall, and she couldn't afford to let him get away.

"I left the burner turned on the lowest setting, thinking sure I'd have time, but…" Despite appearances to the contrary, she tried to sound intelligent, or at least moderately rational.

Fat chance. She sighed. "Look, I've been painting bookcases in the garage and I left the side door open so I could hear the phone, so that's how the smell got into the house, okay? I was just trying to cover it—while I showered—with cinnamon."

"You showered with cinnamon."

Was that skepticism or sympathy? Time to take control. "Yes, well—I probably should have used something heavier than one of those aluminum foil pie pans. Pumpkin. Mrs. Smith's. I hate to throw them away, don't you? They come in handy for scaring deer away from the pittosporum."

Nodding slowly, he backed a few steps closer to the hall door, watching her as if he expected her to hop up on a counter and start flapping her wings. "This *is* the right address, isn't it? Corner of Sugar Lane and Bedlam Boulevard?"

Bedlam Boulevard wasn't even a boulevard, just a plain old street. She'd almost forgotten the developer's love of all things British: Chelsea Circle, Parliament Place, London Lane.

She snickered. And then watched as his lips started to twitch. And then they were both grinning.

Marty said, "Could we start all over, d'you think?"

"I guess maybe we'd better. Cole Stevens. I was told you needed some remodeling done?"

"Martha Owens. I'm mostly called Marty, though. Come on into the living room, the odor shouldn't be so strong there. I'd open a window, but we'd freeze." Ignoring her stinging fingers—she'd probably burned off her fingerprints—Marty led the way, pretending she wasn't barefoot and dripping and utterly devoid of any claim to dignity she might once have possessed.

Following her, Cole wondered if he wouldn't be better off leaving now. He'd never worked for a woman before—at least, not directly.

He wondered if the fact that she was barefoot had anything to do with the way she moved. Hip bone connected to the thigh bone, thigh bone connected to the—

And then he wondered why he was wondering. Why he'd even noticed the way she walked—or the way she'd scrooched up her mouth when she'd hurled that blackened pan outside. For a crazy woman, she was sort of attractive.

It wouldn't hurt to stick around for a few more minutes, seeing as he was here. He hadn't planned on going back to work this soon, but that didn't mean he couldn't change his mind. The one thing he was, was flexible.

When he'd set out earlier this week, he'd had some vague idea of cruising south until he saw someplace that appealed to him. Less than a day out of his old mooring place on the Chesapeake Bay, he'd had some minor engine trouble and looked for a place to lay over. He'd radioed a friend of his, who had recommended Bob Ed's place near the neck of Tull Bay on North Landing River. He'd limped along on one engine, located the place, liked its looks and rented a wet slip for a week, with options.

Yesterday he had exercised his option for another two weeks. One of the things he liked about the place was the fact that, other than a few local commercial fishermen, it was empty. Add to that the fact that, while it was off the beaten track, it was relatively close to a metropolitan area in case he ever needed something that couldn't be found in the sticks.

Hell, there was no law that said he had to keep on running. No family, no job to hold him back. Not much of a reputation either, but the lack of a haircut over the past few months should keep anyone from recognizing him as the whistle-blower who'd brought down the third largest developer in southeastern Virginia.

What he hadn't counted on when he'd pulled up stakes and headed south was having so much time on his hands. When a guy didn't have a real life, things got boring real fast.

He'd been considering moving on when he saw the old guy who ran the place trying to replace a rotten window frame. He'd offered to help, and had been pleased and somewhat surprised to discover that he hadn't quite lost his old skills. By day's end they had replaced three windows on the northeast side of the rambling unpainted building that housed Bob Ed's Ammo, Bait and Tackle, and Guide Service. He'd met Bob Ed's lady, Faylene, briefly yesterday when she'd come to bring a stack of mail from the post office.

Now there was one strange lady. It was largely due to her that he was here today, actually considering signing on for a construction job. Too much fried food had evidently affected his brain.

Either that or too much solitude.

Cole followed the Owens woman into a comfortable, if slightly cluttered living room, where she turned to confront him. He stood six foot two to her five feet plus a few inches, yet she managed to look down her nose at him.

Haughty as a maître d' in a five-star restaurant, she said, "May I see your résumé?"

His résumé. Cole didn't know whether to laugh or to leave. A few minutes ago leaving had seemed the better option, but sooner or later he was going to have to jump-start his career. Living alone aboard his boat with no real structure in his life wasn't going to do it. This job, small as it was, sounded like a good first step if he planned to stay in construction, which was all he knew.

Hands on, though. No more management.

"My résumé," he repeated. He cleared his throat. "Short version—the firm where I worked for the past thirteen years recently went bankrupt, so my résumé would be pretty worthless." He didn't bother to add that the firm had belonged to his ex-father-in-law, who had pushed him into an area of management he had been unprepared for. Deliberately, he'd later learned. The result being that by calling a spade a spade—or in this case, calling a crook a crook—he'd lost his wife, his job, and any ambition he'd once had to be the best damn builder in the business.

"Would I have heard of it?" she asked.

"Were you watching the local news last spring?"

"Local? You mean Muddy Landing?"

He shook his head. "Norfolk. Virginia Beach, specifically." The state line was less than forty-five minutes away. Northeast North Carolina got most of the news from Norfolk feeds.

The way she was eyeing him, she was probably reconsidering her job offer. With no résumé and no referrals, he couldn't blame her, but now that he'd come this far, he was determined not to let that happen. Something about big, cloudy gray eyes and soft, pouty lips…

Oh, hell no. Any decision he made would be based on his

own needs and not on the appeal of any woman. He'd gone that route once before, and look where it had landed him.

"Look, I'll be honest with you," he said.

"For a change?"

Cole didn't particularly like being called a liar, especially when he wasn't, but having been grilled by experts, he let it pass. "I can leave now or we can go on with the interview, your choice," he said quietly. "I'd intended to head on down the Banks and points south in a few days, anyway."

"Then why did you bother to apply?"

Had he thought gray eyes looked soft? At the moment hers looked about as soft as stainless steel. "I'm beginning to wonder," he muttered, half to himself. The lady was as flaky as one of the Colonel's biscuits. "All right, fair question. First, I did a small repair job for a guy who owns the marina where I've been living aboard my boat. Yesterday a friend of his happened to mention that she knew somebody who needed a small remodeling job done in a hurry, and asked if I was interested in earning some maintenance money."

Actually, despite appearances, he had a fairly decent investment income considering his simplified lifestyle. But the market tended to be schizophrenic and, as someone once said, a boat was a hole in the water into which the owner poured money.

"You said that was your first reason. What else? Is there a second reason?"

A second reason. If he said "instinct," she was going to think he was as big a nutcase as she was. As to that, the jury was still out, but until he had more to go on he'd just as soon not have to defend himself.

It had been instinct that had first tipped him off that

Weyrich was dirty. Long before that, it had been instinct that told him Paula was bored with their marriage and looking for bigger fish to fry. Frying them, for all he knew. By that time it had no longer been worth the effort to find out.

"It just struck me as the thing to do," he said finally. "Small town, small job—good place to get my bearings again."

"Again?"

She might look like soft, but the lady was a piranha—big eyes, tousled hair and all. "Look, if it's all the same to you, let's leave my bearings out of this and get on with the business at hand. Do you need a job done, or don't you?"

She took a deep breath, hinting at what lay hidden by a baggy turtleneck sweater that showed signs of age. And he wasn't even a breast man. If anything, he was an eye man, eyes being the window on the soul.

The window on the soul?

Clear case of too much fried food and too much time on his hands.

"It's a remodeling job," she explained. "I doubt if it'll take very long. At least I hope not. I want my downstairs moved upstairs so I can reopen my bookstore downstairs."

Cole thought for a minute, then nodded slowly as a couple of things clicked into place. "The bookshelves you were painting in your garage." The smell still lingered, a combination of burnt cinnamon, fresh urethane and paint thinner—but either his olfactory sense was numbed or the stench was starting to fade.

She nodded. "I thought I'd better refinish them now so that they'll be thoroughly dry by the time my upstairs gets finished so I can move my downstairs upstairs and move the shelves into these two rooms and start restocking."

Okay. He had the general picture now. "You want to

show me what you have in mind?" He hadn't committed himself to anything.

Marty rubbed her right thumb and forefinger together as she considered whether to show him her drawings first or take him upstairs. She'd burned off her fingerprints, which might come in handy in case she couldn't get her bookstore reopened in time and was forced to turn to a life of crime.

"Come on, I'll show you upstairs first so you'll understand my drawings better. You might as well know, you're not the first builder to apply for the job. The others turned it down."

"Any particular reason?" he asked.

Conscious of him just behind her, she made a serious effort not to move her hips any more than she had to. Too much stress was obviously affecting her brain. Just because she'd noticed practically everything about him, from his tarnished brass eyes to the worn areas of his jeans to the way they hugged his quads and glutes and…well, whatever—that didn't mean he was aware of her in any physical sense.

Sasha would have had a field day if she could've tuned in on Marty's thoughts. Her friend was always after her to add a little more vitamin S to her diet. Vitamin sex. "Maybe then," she was fond of saying, "you'd get a decent night's sleep and not be a zombie until noon."

She wasn't that bad. Just because she wasn't a morning person—

He'd asked her a question. He was waiting for an answer. Kick in, brain—it's four-thirty in the afternoon! "Reason why they didn't work out? Well, one never showed up, and the next two, once they found out what I wanted done, told me I was wasting their time. Oh, and one of them said he could only work on weekends because the rest of the time he worked with a building crew at Nags Head." She hadn't yet mentioned the time constraints, but that shouldn't be a problem. It wasn't a major job, after all. Not like starting from scratch and building a house.

"So—here it is." She waved a hand in the general direction of the upstairs hall and the spare bedroom, which she planned to move into so that the larger bedroom could become her living room.

She had painted up here less than two years ago. She'd chosen yellow with white trim on the theory that sunshine colors would help kick-start her brain when she stumbled out of bed and staggered to the bathroom early in the morning.

While he looked around, tapping on walls, studying the ceiling, Marty told herself that it *would* get done. It *was* going to work. Her life was *not* in free fall—it only felt that way because time was wasting. She kept racing her engines but not getting anywhere.

Following him around, she tried not to get her hopes up—tried not to be distracted by the fact that he smelled like leather and something spicy and resinous, and that he looked like—

Well, never mind what he looked like. That had nothing to do with anything except that her social life had been seriously neglected for too long.

They were standing beside the closet she wanted taken out and turned into part of a new kitchen when he said, "You want to show me your drawings now?"

There was plenty of room. It was only her imagination that made it feel as if the walls were shrinking, pushing them closer together. Breathlessly, she said, "Come on, then, but remember, I'm not an architect. You can get the general idea, though." Turning away from her yellow walls, she was aware again of how early it grew dark in late January—especially on cloudy days. "I'll make us some coffee," she said. Heck, she'd cook him a five-course dinner if that was what it took to get him to agree.

Marty saw him glance into the spare bedroom where she'd stored dozens of boxes of paperback books, plus the bulletin boards where she used to tack up cover flats, bookmarks and autographed photos. She hated clutter, always had, and now she was wallowing in the stuff. As Faylene, the housekeeper she could no longer afford, would have said, "You buttered your bread, now lie in it."

Hmm…alone, or with company?

Two

"They're there on the coffee table," Marty said, leaving Cole to look over her plans while she started a pot of coffee. Too late to wish she'd taken time while they were upstairs to pull her hair back with a scrunchy and put on some shoes—and maybe add a dab of her new tinted, coconut-flavored lip balm. Not that she was vain, but darn it, her feet were cold.

Okay, so he was attractive. He wasn't all *that* attractive. Not that she had a type, but if she did, he wasn't it. She'd been married at eighteen to Alan, whose mother had left him this house. Whatever she'd seen in him hadn't lasted much beyond the honeymoon, but as she'd desperately wanted a family, she'd stayed with him. After he'd been diagnosed with MS, leaving was out of the question.

A few years after Alan died she had gotten married again, this time to Beau Conrad, a smooth talker from a wealthy Virginia family—F.F.V., U.D.C. and D.A.R.—all the proper initials. Only, as it turned out, Beau was the black sheep of the family.

Looking back, she could truthfully say that both her husbands had been far handsomer than Cole Stevens. So what was so intriguing about shabby clothes, shaggy hair, and features that could best be described as rugged? Was she all that starved for masculine attention?

Evidently she was. When she'd first mentioned her building plans, Sasha had offered to buy her a stud-finder. Four-times-divorced Sasha, ever the optimist. It had taken Marty several minutes to realize that her friend wasn't talking about one of those gadgets you used to find a safe place to hammer a nail into a wall.

"You see what I mean, don't you?" she called now from the kitchen. There'd been no sounds from the living room for the past several minutes. "Where I want the closet taken out and added to the back wall to make room for a couple of counters and whatever else I need for a small kitchen." She could mention the plumbing and wiring later. She didn't want to scare him off until she had him on the hook. She was rapidly running out of time. If it didn't happen with this one, she might not make the deadline, in which case she might as well have a humongous yard sale, sell off her remaining stock and then look for a job in an area where there weren't any. Either that or pull up stakes and move, which wasn't an option. The closest thing to roots she had was this house. Beau had tried to force her to sell it, but she'd held out. God knows, it was about the only thing of hers he hadn't forced her to sell. The paintings and antiques he'd inherited from his own family had been sold off soon after they'd married, along with the few nice things she'd been able to accumulate.

Damn his lying, thieving hide. She hoped wherever he was now, he was married to some bimbo who would take him for every cent he had.

Marty laid a Tole tray with two mugs, sugar, half-and-half and a plate of biscotti. As a bribe, it wasn't much, but at the moment it was the best she could do.

"Of course, I guess I could always get a camp stove and a dorm refrigerator," she said as she joined him in the living room. "It's not like I did a lot of entertaining."

No comment. Was that a good sign or a bad sign? At least he hadn't walked out after seeing her drawings. The stick figures might have been overkill. Occasionally in moments of desperation she got carried away.

"I guess we need to discuss money," she said, searching his face for a clue. If knocking out a wall or two and putting in a kitchen on the second floor was going to cost too much, she might have to—

Might have to do what? Open her bookstore in the garage? It wasn't even insulated, much less heated.

So then what, rob a bank? Get a loan? She hated debt with a vengeance, having been in it for one reason or another most of her adult life.

He'd taken off his leather bomber jacket. Good sign or not?

Who knows. The Sphinx was a chatterbox compared to Cole Stevens. He wore a faded blue oxford-cloth dress shirt with frayed collar, and turned back his cuffs to reveal a pair of bronzed, muscular forearms lightly furred with dark, wiry hair. She couldn't help but notice his hands, but then, she always noticed a man's hands. They said almost as much about him as his shoes. Shoes were something she had noticed ever since hearing her friend Daisy, who was a geriatric nurse, talk about this doctor who wore neat three-piece suits and silk ties, but whose nails were dirty and whose shoes were always in need of a polish. It turned out that for years he'd been killing off his elderly patients.

Okay, so his carpenter's deck shoes weren't the kind you polished. They were old, but obviously top-of-the-line. He had nice hands with clean nails, and she liked the way he handled her drawing pad, treating it as though the drawings had real value.

How would those hands feel on a woman's body? It had been so long....

Breathe through your mouth, idiot, your brain's obviously starved for oxygen!

She waited for him to speak—to say either "This looks doable," or "No thanks, I'll pass." The faded blue of his shirt made his skin look tan, which made his hair look even lighter on top and darker underneath. She was almost positive the tan was real and not the product of a bottle. Sasha, who was a hair person, could tell in a minute, but Marty didn't want Sasha to get even a glimpse of this guy. Her redheaded friend was a Pied Piper where men were concerned, and Marty intended to keep this one around for as long as it took.

For as long as it took for what?

To finish the job on schedule, fool!

"I didn't know if you took anything in your coffee," she said when he finally glanced up.

Despite a lap full of drawings, he'd made an effort to rise when she'd come in. She'd shaken her head, indicating that he should sit. Obediently, he'd sat, knees spread apart so that what Sasha called his "package" was evident.

You are not *having a hot flash! You're nowhere near ready for menopause!*

"Black's fine," he said, and took a sip of coffee.

"I could open another window. The rain's let up," she said. The odor inside was still pretty awful.

"No need," he said, and went on studying her drawings.

Hopefully he hadn't noticed her burning cheeks. "The stick figures are silly, I know," she said in a rush. "I was just doodling. Sort of—you know, illustrating me washing dishes, leaning over to use the under-the-counter fridge. Anything you don't understand, I can explain." That is, she could if she could manage to get her brain back online.

"They're clear enough. Thing is," he said, "this right here is a weight-bearing wall. I'll need to leave at least three feet of it, but then I can open your entryway right here and shift this wall down to here."

She forced her eyes to focus on the area he was indicating instead of his pointer finger. Then, because they needed to share the same vantage point if they were to discuss her drawings, Marty left her platform rocker and settled onto the sofa beside him.

Even without the bomber jacket he smelled sort of leathery with intriguing overtones. Salt water, sunshine and one of those subtle aftershave lotions that were babe magnets.

"Mmm, what was that?"

"I said the space can be better utilized if you don't mind using part of the closet for your range and oven. Stacking units would fit."

Marty realized their shoulders were touching—in fact, she was leaning against him. She sat up straight, but as he outweighed her by at least fifty pounds, she had to struggle to overcome the slope of the cushion.

Damn sofa. She'd never liked the thing, anyway. Sasha

had bought it at a huge discount for a customer who also hadn't liked it, so she'd let Marty have it at cost.

"Well," she said brightly, wriggling her butt away from his until she could hang on to the padded arm. "Uh, there are a couple more things we need to talk about. That is, if you're still interested in taking the job."

Cole flexed his shoulders and tried not to breathe too deeply. Yeah, he was still interested in taking on the job. Construction jobs were plentiful all up and down the nearby Outer Banks, but then, Muddy Landing was undergoing a small building boom as more and more Virginians moved south of the border. And while wages might be higher on the Banks, working conditions, especially in January, could be a lot worse. Climbing all over a three-story building some fifty or more feet above ground level, with a howling wind threatening to blow him out into the Atlantic? No, thanks. If he had to relearn the building trade after more than a decade in management, he'd sooner start out in a slightly more protected environment, even if his employer did happen to be a bit of a flake.

"The first man who answered my ad told me the job was a boondoggle. I'm not exactly sure what he meant. Actually, I'm not even sure what a boondoggle is, and words are my business—in a manner of speaking. Something to do with the government, I guess."

Cole had to smile—something he hadn't done too much of in the recent past. "I think it's a general description of most bureaucracies. You mentioned time constraints?" He reached for another biscotti—his third. The things were meant for dunking, but he figured he didn't know her well enough for dunking, so he bit off a chunk and tried to catch the crumbs in the palm of his hand.

"Right. There's this deadline," she said earnestly. "New zoning laws go into effect the middle of March, and unless I'm in business before then, I won't be grandfathered. That means—"

"I know what it means."

"Yes, well—of course you do. See, there are already several businesses in the neighborhood, but they won't allow any new ones to open after the fifteenth."

She hooked her bare toes on the edge of the coffee table, then dropped them to the floor again. She kept rubbing her thumb and forefinger together like a crapshooter calling up his mojo. Her eyes darted to the clock, and she bit her lip.

"Ms. Owens, are you sure this is what you want to do? Tear up your house so you can open—what, a bookstore?"

"I have to," she said simply. Then, with another glance at the clock, she quickly explained about Marty's New and Used. "Up until last fall I rented a two-room cinder-block building that used to be a garage and a bait-and-tackle shop and some other things. Anyway, the rent was cheap enough and the location was okay, I guess, but the income still couldn't keep up with the overhead. Some days I didn't even sell a single book." She gave up rubbing her fingers and folded her hands together, resting them on her knees. Her toes were back on the coffee table. "So I thought if I reopened here, I'd at least save the rent because I own my house. It's all paid off. My first husband inherited it from his mama."

Whoa. Her first husband? He was nowhere near ready to share personal histories.

The third time he caught her looking at the clock he asked her if she had a problem.

"Not really, but there's this dog I walk twice a day. I'm running late today because I was waiting for—"

She hesitated, and he filled in the blanks. She'd been waiting for him to show up.

"For the rain to stop," she finished.

The rain had stopped. A few chinks of salmon-pink sunset broke through the dark clouds.

Cole said, "Then why don't I leave you to it? I need to run a few errands if I'm going to stick around the area."

She looked so hopeful, he could have kicked himself. They hadn't even reached a concrete agreement yet.

"Are you? Going to stick around, I mean? Like I said, if things don't work out just right, I'm stuck with a garage full of bookshelves and a spare room filled with thousands of used paperbacks."

"Two things we still need to talk about—your deadline and my wages."

Looking entirely too hopeful, she said, "When can you give me an estimate?"

If he didn't watch it, Cole told himself, those big gray eyes of hers were going to influence his decision. That was no way to start rebuilding a career. "How about we both think it over tonight and I come back first thing in the morning with an estimate. If we reach an agreement, I can start right away. I should be able to bring it in on schedule, depending on how much time you need after the job's completed."

They both stood. Her eyes and her ivory complexion and delicate features called to mind the word fragile, yet he had a feeling she was nowhere near as fragile as she looked.

She said, "Come for breakfast. You're not organic or vegan or anything like that, are you?"

"Methodist, but sort of lapsed," he replied gravely, and heard a gurgle of laughter that invited a like response. He managed to hold it to a brief smile.

They agreed on a time and she saw him to the door and said she'd see him in the morning. It sounded more like a question than a statement, but he didn't reply. He had some serious thinking to do before he made a commitment. One thing for certain—he was nowhere near ready for retirement. As to what he was going to do with the rest of his life and where he was going to do it, that was still up for grabs.

Standing in the doorway, Marty watched as the most intriguing man she'd met in years adjusted his steps to her flagstones. She sighed. What a strikingly attractive man— and yet he wasn't really handsome. It was something else. Something in the way he carried himself, the way he…

Maybe Sasha was right and she was seriously deficient when it came to vitamin S.

Mutt was all over her the minute she opened his gate at the kennel. His owners, the Hallets, who lived three streets over in the development that had grown up around Alan's mother's old house back in the seventies, were on a two-week cruise out of Norfolk. Marty was being paid to pick Mutt up twice a day for a run, as the space provided by the boarding kennel hardly sufficed for a big, shaggy clown that looked as if he might be part St. Bernard, part Clydesdale.

"Whoa, get off my foot, you big ox." She managed to snap on his choke collar while he did his best to trip her up. He'd started barking the minute he saw her, and didn't let up until she opened the front door. Then he nearly pulled her off her feet trying to get outside.

She gave him a full half hour because that was what she'd agreed to do. Not a minute less, but not a minute more this time because she had to have him back by six when the kennel closed for the day. If she missed the deadline she'd have no choice but to take the crazy dog home with her, and that would be disastrous.

There had to be an easier way to earn money. If she were a diver she could drive to Manteo to the aquarium every day and scrub the alligators or maybe floss the sharks' teeth. Unfortunately, her marketable skills weren't all that impressive in a town where, other than flipping hamburgers, jobs were practically handed down from father to son. None of Muddy Landing's farming, fishing and hunting applied to her.

Maybe she and Sasha could start charging for their matchmaking services. Practically everyone in town knew what they were up to, anyway. It was no big secret; they'd been at it too long. They'd been good at it, too—Daisy, Sasha and Marty, with occasional input from Faylene, the housekeeper they'd all shared for years until Marty had gone out of business and Daisy had unexpectedly fallen in love with a good-looking guy who'd come east in search of his roots. A nurse and easily the most sensible of the trio, Daisy had fallen head over heels and ended up marrying Kell and moving to Oklahoma.

Marty and her friends had been good at it, though—all the planning and finagling it took to bring two people together. Three of their most recent matches had actually ended in marriage and two more couples were still involved.

Of course, there'd been a few spectacular failures, too, but it had been great fun. Mostly they'd been forgiven their blunders.

But Sasha was up to her ears in her latest decorating project, so matchmaking was taking a time-out. "And that just leaves me," Marty panted as she struggled to hang on to the end of the leash. She was wearing out her last pair of cross-trainers trying to keep up with Super Mutt. "Slow down, will you? Let me catch my breath!"

If she hurried, she might get home before he left for the day.

Right. Looking like she'd just finished a five-mile run. That would really impress the heck out of Cole, wouldn't it?

By the time Cole got back to the small marina with a take-out supper consisting of barbecue, fries, hush puppies and slaw, the last vestige of daylight had faded. And second thoughts were stacking up fast. Not about the work itself, although it had been a while since he'd done any actual construction work. That wasn't what had him worried.

As he stepped aboard his aged thirty-one-foot cabin cruiser, he waved to Bob Ed, who was outside sorting through a stack of decoys under the mercury-vapor security light.

The friendly guide called across the intervening space, "You see her?"

"I saw her."

"Ya gonna do it?"

"We're still negotiating," Cole called back.

Nodding, Bob Ed went back to checking out his canvasbacks. He was a man of few words. Which was just as well, Cole thought, amused, as Bob Ed's better half appeared to be a woman of many. Cole had met her only briefly, but she'd made an indelible impression.

What bothered him, Cole admitted to himself once he was inside, the lights on and his small space heater thawing out the damp cold, was the Owens woman. Or rather, his reaction to her. Before meeting her he would have sworn he was permanently immunized. Trouble was, Marty Owens and Paula Weyrich Stevens, his high-maintenance ex-wife, were two different species. If Paula had ever lifted a hand to do anything more strenuous than polish her nails, he'd missed it. Even for that she usually depended on a manicurist. Paula's idea of a perfect day started at noon with a three-daiquiri lunch at the club, followed by a shopping marathon, followed by dinner out with whatever poor sucker she could reel in to escort her while her poor slob of a husband worked late. Actually, Cole had been consumed those late nights with digging into the mess at Weyrich, Inc.

Marty Owens, on the other hand, varnished bookshelves in her spare time and tried to cover the smell by setting a pan of cinnamon on fire. She walked a friend's dog—at least, Cole assumed she did it for a friend. If she was hard up enough to do it for money, she probably couldn't afford the remodeling job she wanted done.

On the other hand, if she didn't get it done, what would happen to her business? Reading between the lines, he could only conclude that she was pretty close to the edge. And, like a certain ex-builder he could name, looking for the best way to revive a career that had collapsed through no fault of her own.

Not that he could swear to that last, but from what he'd seen so far, Ms. Owens was industrious, intelligent and not afraid to get her hands dirty. The fact that she was also sexy without making a big deal out of it wasn't a factor in any decision he might make. No way.

Definitely not.

As for the demise of his own career, Cole freely accepted the blame. All he'd had to do was turn a blind eye to what he'd uncovered—the good-old-boy bidding system, the under-the-table payoffs, the shoddy workmanship that had eventually resulted in three deaths and a number of injuries when the second floor of a parking garage collapsed due to insufficient reinforcement.

Oh, yeah, he'd blown the whistle on Joshua Weyrich, but by that time his marriage to Paula was washed up anyway. Looking back, about the only thing he and Paula had ever had in common was a serious case of raging hormones. Once that had died a natural death, there'd been nothing left to sustain a relationship. The only reason they'd stayed together as long as they had was that breaking up required more time and energy than either of them was willing to spend.

But once he'd blown the whistle on her father, détente had ended. He had gladly ceded to Paula the showy house they'd been given as a wedding present, plus all furnishings, including the baby grand piano she didn't play, the art collection she never bothered to look at and a bunch of custom-made furniture designed not for comfort but to impress.

With the help of a good lawyer, Cole had managed to keep his boat, his old Guild guitar, his fishing gear and roughly half his investments—which was all he really needed. He considered himself damn lucky to walk away with that much.

Now he looked around for a place to set his supper. The fold-down table was covered with fishing tackle. He made room for the take-out plate and a cold beer, shucked off his shoes and slid onto the bench. To say his living quarters were compact was putting it generously, but then, he didn't need much space. The wet slip, utilities included, cost a lot less than he'd been paying at his old place on the Chesapeake Bay.

He turned on the twelve-inch TV and caught up on the news while he ate. When the talking heads turned to the latest celebrity trial, Cole's thoughts drifted back to the woman he'd just met. After hearing about the job prospect from Bob Ed and his lady, Ms. Beasley—mostly from the lady—he hadn't known what to expect. Julia Roberts with big gray eyes and a brown squirrel's nest dripping down her back didn't fit the image he'd conjured up when he'd spoken with her briefly on the phone.

When she'd asked to see his references, he'd mentioned Bob Ed.

"Any reason why I should trust your word?" she'd asked.

The answer, of course, was that she shouldn't—but if she didn't know it, he wasn't about to tell her. If he'd learned one thing from the mess he'd been involved in over the past eighteen months, it was to listen to his instincts.

And right now his internal weather vane was telling him there was more at stake here than just a chance to see if he could still do the work. Without bothering to think further, he grabbed a paper napkin and started listing the tools he'd need to buy.

Halfway through the list his mind began to wander, distracted by thoughts of a pair of gray eyes, and the way they could go so quickly from suspicion to amusement to…interest?

Three

Sasha showed up for breakfast with a box of Krispy Kremes and a copy of *Architectural Digest*. "Check out page sixty-eight and think about the color scheme for your front room. I'm headed to Norfolk—just thought I'd stop by on my way." Her cheeks were pink from exposure to the damp, cold air, her eyes avid for anything that even hinted at romance.

While Marty was still trying to nudge her brain awake, her early morning visitor planted beringed fists on her rounded hips and said, "Let's hear it. Start from the first and don't leave out anything. If he's as prime as Faylene says he is, we might want to add him to our list. Is he taller than five-ten? Because Lily Sullivan over on Chelsea Circle is at least that. She towers over me, even in my new green Jimmys. I'm thinking of finding someone shorter to do my taxes. It's bad enough to be intimidated by the IRA without—" She blinked a battery of fake lashes and said plaintively, "Wha-a-at? Oh, Lord, you're still sleepwalking, aren't you."

Still wading through her usual morning fog, Marty refused to be intimidated by the five-foot-three-inch steamroller. "Look, I've got a date with a dog, so make this fast. Exactly what do you mean by 'prime,' and what difference does it make what he looks like?"

"Actually, none, I guess. We just thought—that is, Faye said—and I was thinking that if he was going to be hanging around long enough to destroy your second floor and put it back together again, he might like to join in a few social activities. You know what they say, 'all work and no play'?"

Marty sighed. "It bugs you, doesn't it? The fact that somewhere in three counties there's a competent, independent woman who gets along perfectly without the benefit of a man. Did it ever occur to you that some of us like our lives just fine the way they are?"

The redheaded interior designer tried looking innocent and gave it up as a lost cause. "You're talking like you never did any matchmaking. How about Clarice and Eddie? How about Sadie Glover down at the ice-cream parlor and—"

"How about stuffing a doughnut in it?" Marty poured coffee, adding half-and-half—which her guest called diet cream—to both mugs. "Mutt's waiting, so eat fast."

"Gross. Do you have one of those scoopy things in case he does his business in somebody's yard?"

Marty rolled her eyes. "Sash, I really need to get this job done in record time, and once y'all start messing around with my carpenter, you're going to scare him off—so quit it, okay? Just knock it off. At least wait until I'm finished with him."

Sasha began licking the sugar coating off another doughnut. "Just thinking about poor lonesome Lily, that's all. I ran into her at the post office the other day and she happened to mention that she hadn't had a date since last summer."

"Just happened to mention it, huh? Like you didn't pry it out of her with a crowbar?"

"Would I do that? Anyway, we're running short of bachelors and I thought I'd get your take on whatshisname, your new carpenter. So? What's he like? Faylene says he's a hunk."

"Dreadlocks, whiskers, ragged Brooks Brothers shirt, worn-out L.L. Bean shoes and no calluses. Which probably means he buys his clothes at a thrift shop using money he stole instead of working for it."

"You jest." Sasha licked her fingers, showing off inch-long nails and a glittering array of jewelry.

"I jest not. I might exaggerate now and then—I might even occasionally speculate—but please, Sash, don't go trying to distract my carpenter. He's my last chance."

"No problem, hon, he's all yours during business hours. Did you say he was tall?"

"Let's just say he's taller than you are."

"Everybody over the age of twelve is taller than I am. Is he good looking?" She wriggled her generous curves. "Faye says—"

Marty hesitated just a second too long, and Sasha pounced. "He is! Admit it, you're hot for him and you don't want him exposed to Lily until you've had time to make an impression on him yourself."

"Will you *stop it?* It's nothing like that! He's supposed to come by to give me an estimate early this morning, and I've got to walk Mutt first and get back here—so if you don't mind, you need to leave now and so do I. Five minutes ago, in fact."

Sasha grinned, her eyes sparkling like faceted gemstones. Today they were aquamarine. Tomorrow, they might be topaz or sapphire. The woman had never met an artifice she didn't adore, regardless of the time of day.

Marty, on the other hand, was barely able to find her mouth with a toothbrush, even after she'd stood under the shower for five minutes. A morning person she was not. The time had long since come and gone when she could stay up half the night reading and wake up bright-eyed and bushy-tailed at the crack of dawn.

"Look, just let me get him on the hook and then you and Faye can have your way with him. All I want is his skills."

"What else is there?" the redhead murmured.

"His carpentry skills!" Marty all but shouted.

"Shh, calm down, honey—no need to get all excited. You can have him during working hours, but Faylene and I want whatever's left over for Lily. She needs a little R 'n' R before the tax rush starts. We tried Egbert on her, but it didn't work out."

In the middle of a jaw-cracking yawn, Marty had to laugh. She edged her best friend toward the front door. "No kidding. I wonder why?"

"Hey, when you're wired for one-ten, you don't go fooling around with two-twenty. I learned that from husband number two, the electrical engineer."

"I thought number two was the con man."

"Aren't they all?" Sasha called cheerfully over her shoulder.

Marty watched her friend sashay down the flagstone walk hitting about every third flagstone, not even bothering to look where she was going. That was Sasha—stiletto heels, red leggings and faux fur at a quarter of eight on a cold, gray Monday morning, leaving in her wake a trail of Nettie Rosenstein's Odalisque. She might look purely ornamental, but when she was on a job, she worked harder than any woman Marty knew—including Faylene, Muddy Landing's unchallenged queen of housecleaning.

As soon as the red Lexus convertible disappeared around the corner, Marty grabbed a coat and a pair of gloves. Cole had said he'd be here between eight-thirty and nine, which barely gave her enough time for Mutt's half-hour gallop.

"You'll make it, easy," she assured herself as she waited for her cold engine to turn over. "Think positive," that was her motto. It had to be, because any negative thinking might send her into a serious decline.

There were several doughnuts left in the box. Still breathless from the dog walk—or in Mutt's case, dog gallop—Marty left them on the table as she hurriedly washed the mugs and turned them down in the dish drainer. A moment later she heard the truck pull into the driveway behind her minivan, which meant she'd run out of time. Her hair was a wild, windblown tangle, her nose and cheeks red from the cold, and there was no time to dash upstairs for a quick fix.

Probably just as well. No point in giving him the wrong impression. Inhaling deeply of the air that now smelled only faintly of varnish and burnt spice, she braced herself for bad news. It was called hedging her bets. Deliberately not getting her hopes up. If so-and-so happens, she always reasoned, I can always do such-and-such, and if that doesn't work out, I'll just fall back on my contingency plan.

What contingency plan? This *was* her contingency plan.

She opened the front door before he could knock. "Good morning, have you had breakfast?"

He raised his eyebrows. They were almost, but not quite black. Thick, but not unkempt. "Did I misunderstand? I thought—"

Oh, shoot. She'd told him to come by for breakfast. "The bacon's ready to pop in the frying pan, the eggs ready to scramble and there's doughnuts to start with. Toss your coat on the bench or hang it on the rack and come on into the kitchen."

Oh, my mercy, he looked even better than she remembered! She was no expert, but after two husbands and several near misses, she'd learned a few things about men. For instance, she knew the really handsome ones were about as deep as your average oil slick, having spent a lifetime getting by on their looks. Cole Stevens wasn't that handsome. Whatever it was that made him stand out from all the men she'd ever met, it was far more potent than a pleasant arrangement of features.

"Do you have a phone where I can reach you if I need to?" she asked.

He gave her his cell phone number and she hastily scratched it down on the bottom of a grocery list. Then he followed her into the kitchen.

"Warming up out there," he said. It wasn't.

"Spring's on the way," she replied. It wasn't. "Where are you staying, in case something comes up and I need to reach you?"

"At this place down by the river. Bob Ed's. I thought I mentioned it yesterday—I'm living aboard my boat at the moment."

Right. Bob Ed and Faylene had sent him, after all. There'd been a few distractions yesterday, including the man himself.

"Isn't it cold?"

"Yep."

And that was the end of that…unless she wanted to invite him to move into her warm, insulated house, which wasn't even a distant possibility.

Back to business. "How long do you think it will take to tear out what needs tearing out and turn my upstairs hall into a kitchen?" She placed three strips of bacon in a frying pan and turned on the burner. At the first whiff of smoke she remembered to turn on the fan. The cover and batteries for her smoke detector were still on the counter where she'd left them.

Spotting them, Cole replaced the batteries and clicked the cover in place.

Marty smiled her thanks. "I was just getting ready to do that," she lied.

"As to the tear-down, it shouldn't take more than a day or two."

Was that a yes, he'd do it, or an answer to a rhetorical question? Forcing herself not to sound too eager, she said, "That sounds great."

He stood beside the table staring out the window, his hands tucked halfway into the hip pockets of his jeans as the tantalizing aroma of frying bacon filled the room.

"Forecast is calling for more rain," he said.

Marty glanced over her shoulder. *Oh my, honey, I hate to tell you this, but those jeans are a little overcrowded.* "It'll be February in a few more days, and after that, March—that's when spring starts for real. Of course, we get those Hatteras Lows that can hang around for days, beating the devil out of any blossom that dares show its face."

"Mmm-hmm," he murmured.

Mr. Enigma. The fact that Marty tried not to look at him again didn't mean she wasn't aware of him with every cell in her undernourished body.

She took up the bacon and placed the strips on a folded paper towel. Whipping a dab of *salsa con queso* into the eggs, she tried to focus her mind on the estimate and not on the man. The fact that he'd showed up meant he was ready to talk business. Whether or not she could afford him without taking out a loan remained to be seen.

"Have a seat. D'you need to wash up first? The bathroom's upstairs—but you know that, of course. Or you can use the sink down here if you'd rather. The hand towel's clean—or there's paper."

Excuse me and my big, blathering mouth, I always talk like this when I'm on the verge of losing my mind.

A few minutes later, Marty popped two slices of bread in the toaster and filled two plates. Cole had excused himself and gone upstairs, either to wash up or to take another look at the job before committing himself. Thank goodness she'd made her bed as soon as she'd crawled out of it. Was her gown hanging behind the bathroom door? Had she put the cap back on the toothpaste?

Well, shoot, did it matter? At least she was wearing

shoes and socks today. He had no way of knowing she just happened to be wearing the only pair of jeans she'd ever owned that cost more than a hundred bucks. She'd bought them on sale two years ago, just to prove something or other to Sasha—she'd forgotten now what it was.

"I've got strawberry jam, marmalade and homemade fig preserves," she told her guest when he came back downstairs. "Help yourself."

Hope for the best, prepare for the worst, that was her motto. He would hardly eat her food if he intended to turn down the job, now would he? Or price himself out of the market. Unless he was broke and hungry or totally lacking in ethics.

He might be broke, and he was certainly hungry, judging by the way he was packing away his breakfast—but she'd be willing to bet on his ethics. Something about the way he looked her square in the eye told her that much.

Right. And Beau hadn't looked her in the eye and lied like a rug?

A few minutes later he laid his knife and fork across the top of his plate, poured himself another half cup of coffee and then held the pot over her cup. "It looks feasible."

Not wanting to have to excuse herself and race to the bathroom, Marty declined the coffee. They were finally getting down to brass tacks. "Feasible?" she prompted.

He nodded. "That wall you want removed—I think I mentioned yesterday it's a weight-bearing wall. Structurally, you need it, but I can work around it and still get your basic needs taken care of if you're willing to compromise."

"Compromise is my middle name."

Her basic needs? If he had the slightest idea of what

her basic needs were at this moment, he'd hit the road running. She hadn't even realized she had any basic needs until he'd shown up on her doorstep yesterday— or rather, when he'd burst into her house, yelling for a fire extinguisher.

Forget the fire extinguisher; bring on the cold shower.

"Does this mean you're going to do it?" she ventured.

"You want an hourly rate or an estimate for the complete job?"

"Um…whichever you'd rather."

"Then how about this?" He fingered a folded piece of paper from his shirt pocket—Brooks Brothers again, frayed collar, white oxford cloth, button missing three down from the top. Why did she have to notice every tiny detail about the man? Because she was a Virgo?

Ha. A Virgo with her Venus in Scorpio. According to that article she'd read recently she was supposed to be repressed, but secretly obsessed by sex, which just showed how much stock you could put in all that astrology bunk.

Cautiously, she unfolded the note. The first thing that caught her eye was his handwriting. Or rather, his printing. Actually, it was a combination. Sort of masculine with unexpected grace notes. Like the man himself, she thought before she could stop herself.

His silence weighed on her, making her aware that he was waiting for some reaction. "I don't see any real problem," she said finally.

No real problem if you didn't count her entire nest egg disappearing down a sinkhole. But then, what were nest eggs for? Once hers hatched she could start accumulating eggs all over again. Or if not, she could always sell her house, buy a tent and a bicycle and move to the beach, where summer jobs were plentiful.

"Then," he said, "shall we both sign it, date it and call it a deal?"

Hearing the crunch of tires on her driveway the next morning, Marty fought off a fresh set of misgivings. It was going to cost a bundle and there was no guarantee things would work out in the end. If she could fail in a stand-alone bookstore on the edge of Muddy Landing's tiny shopping district, she could fail even faster in a residential location.

She'd spent the morning moving out of her bedroom and into the smaller spare room. Compared to wrestling all those heavy bookshelves, dismantling a double bed, dragging it into the next room and setting it up again was child's play. She'd learned a long time ago how to lift without endangering any vital organs.

A few backaches didn't count. Life was full of little backaches.

She slid the mattress across the hardwood floor and flopped it onto the box springs just as she heard Cole call up the stairs.

"The door was unlocked, so I came on in. Okay?"

She'd mentioned yesterday that if she wasn't here when he came to work, the front door would be unlocked. He hadn't said anything, but from his expression, she gathered he didn't think it was a good idea.

"This is Muddy Landing," she'd told him. "Crime rate zilch, if you don't count the occasional kids' pranks. But if it makes you feel any safer, I'll start locking the door whenever I leave."

He'd nodded and said that would be safer.

"If you get here before I get back from walking the dog, the key will be under the doormat."

He'd rolled his eyes. Greeny gold eyes, thick black eyelashes, not-quite-bushy black brows. *Be still my heart.*

"Come on up," she called downstairs. "I just finished clearing out the big bedroom." Without thinking, she massaged her lower back with both hands. Occasionally when she was in a hurry she still forgot to lift with her legs.

It took two trips to bring up his tools. He handed her a roll of heavy-duty trash bags. "This first part's going to be messy. I thought about renting a Shop-Vac, but—"

"Oh, I already have one," she said proudly as if she'd just produced the winning lottery number.

"Great. I figure I can reuse most of the studs and rafters, but the rest—"

She nodded vigorously. "I know, plasterboard walls can't be reused. Will we have to take down the ceiling where the wall comes out?"

"First, let's settle this 'we' business. I work alone."

"Oh, but I—"

"My way or no way. I do the cleanup as I go along. If it's not clean enough for you, you can do it over again while I'm on a break."

"But I—"

"Marty—Ms. Owens, I agreed to do the job. I did not agree to have to explain everything I do and then have to argue over whether or not I could have done it another way. I doubt if you have enough insurance—the right kind, at least—to compensate either of us when I trip over you and we both break a few bones."

She took a deep breath, trying her best to ignore the hint of aftershave, laundry soap and something essentially masculine. Dammit, you'd think an aching back would be enough of a distraction. "I only wanted to help."

"Don't. I know what needs doing, I know how to do it. What I'm not good at is having my concentration broken every few minutes by questions."

She felt like telling him he was fired, but she didn't dare. They had signed a contract...sort of. Besides, if she were honest with herself—and she always tried to be—she didn't want him to leave. He was her last hope. He was also...

Well. That was irrelevant. He was her employee, period. They'd settle later which one of them was in charge.

She was backing toward the stairs when the phone rang. It was still sitting on the floor in the bedroom she'd just vacated. Bending at the knees rather than risking further injury to her back, she scooped it up, keeping one eye on Cole Stevens, who was tapping walls just a few feet away.

"Oh, hi, Faylene." With a sigh, she leaned against the wall, resigned to listening as the long-winded friend who had also, until recently, been her once-a-week housekeeper, described the yacht that had recently berthed at the marina just south of Bob Ed's place.

"Two men's all I seen, but we could have us a boatload of 'em. If they're still here for Bob Ed's party Sunday night, I'm thinking 'bout askin' 'em over."

Marty made some appropriate response, which wasn't really necessary. Once Faylene got the bit between her teeth, she was off and running.

"She's one o' these fancy yachts with the kind of old-fashioned woodwork you don't see much anymore. You think I should invite 'em to the goose-stew?"

The goose-stew. Once the holidays were over, stews, fries and candy-boils constituted the main social events until box-supper season. "Why not? No point in wasting a yacht-load of men," she said jokingly.

"That's what I thought. How's your man working out?"

"My—? Faylene, he's not my man!"

"That's what I'm talking about. If the one I sent you don't work out, maybe we can gaff you one of these."

Marty sighed heavily. "Invite them all, married or single. It's up to you." *Just so you leave my carpenter alone,* she added silently.

She listened for a few more minutes while Faylene speculated about all the things an unmarried yachtsman might have in common with either a bookseller or an accountant, most of her ideas being gleaned from various soap operas. Faye was as bad as Sasha when it came to dishing and conniving.

Leaning against the bedroom wall, Marty held the phone away from her ear while she absently rubbed her burnt fingertips together. All the boxes of books she'd shifted from one bedroom to the other still had to be hauled downstairs again. She'd have left them in the garage, but dampness was a book's worst enemy.

When Faylene paused for breath, Marty said, "Okay, hon, invite the entire crew and let the games begin." She hung up quickly before her friend could launch another barrage.

After Daisy had moved, the housekeeper had slipped into the matchmaking trio as if she'd always been a part of it. Actually, she had—even after their misguided effort to match her up with the mechanic, Gus Mathias, had failed so spectacularly.

Rather than risk her back by bending over again, Marty

pulled the phone cord from the wall. Was there a jack in the spare room? If not, she needed to have one installed.

Glancing up, she caught Cole watching her, his expression guarded. "I've got some errands to run," she said. "I'll just put the Shop-Vac at the bottom of the stairs and you can get it whenever you need it, okay?"

He might never win any Mr. Congeniality awards, she told herself on the way to the supermarket, but he was hers, bought and paid for.

Or if not bought and paid for, at least signed and delivered.

Four

Cole waited until he heard her go downstairs before taking down the rest of the crown molding and setting it inside the bedroom she'd recently vacated. The room still carried that subtle fragrance he'd quickly come to associate with the woman. Not polyurethane and fried cinnamon. Nothing overt, like Paula's, but something that reminded him of the kind of flowers you might catch a whiff of while cruising in the tropics on a hot summer evening.

This is Muddy Landing, you jerk. It's January, so cut it out and get back to work.

Replaying her phone conversation in his mind, Cole thought, that was fast work. Some poor guy ties up at a marina and already the local ladies were swarming like sirens. Maybe he should stop by and pass on a word of warning, one sailor to another.

Or maybe he should mind his own business.

What was it she'd said? *Let the games begin?*

He hated to think Marty was involved in that kind of game, but it was none of his business. His job was to do what he'd contracted to do, collect his wages and move on to the next marina, the next job—maybe the next country.

He heard a door shut downstairs as he unscrewed another switch plate and set it aside. He had already taken down one section of plasterboard.

He figured her bungalow for late fifties or early sixties, several decades older than the other houses in the development. Back when this one was built, two bedrooms and a single bath were enough for most young couples. If the family outgrew the original floorplan, they usually built on an addition. That was before the days of starter homes.

But it was her house. She could do what she wanted with it, including turn it into a bookstore. Just because he'd moved out of a five-bedroom, four-bath plastic palace into a boat so small you had to go up on deck to change your mind—

Time to quit thinking so damn much about the house and its owner. Time to do the job he'd been hired to do, then move on.

Before he'd married the boss's daughter and graduated to a corner office where he'd been anchored to a damn desk, Cole had done just about every kind of construction work there was, starting with the boatyard where he'd landed his first summer job. But it had been years since he'd done any hands-on carpentry other than helping Bob Ed with those windows, and the hours he put in on the *Time Out*.

Maybe this had been a mistake. Maybe he should have moved on, waited for more time to pass. He was permanently immunized against sophisticated high-maintenance women who used their sexuality as bargaining chips.

But when it came to the kind of beauty that didn't rely on paint and polish, he might be just a tad susceptible.

What do you bet, he asked himself, amused, that underneath those baggy clothes she's wearing plain white cotton underwear?

The next few hours passed quickly while he measured, marked and cut, his thoughts occasionally straying from the job at hand. Funny how quickly he'd gotten comfortable with her after that near calamity he'd walked in on yesterday. He usually took his time getting to know people. Even before his career, not to mention his personal life, had imploded, he had never been known for his sociability.

Don't get too attached to the place, he warned himself. He happened to like solid, unpretentious houses, and he appreciated those same qualities in a woman—but this was just another job. That was *all* it was.

Still, she was solid and unpretentious, and more. Intelligent but without making an issue of it. If those crazy little stick figures were any indication, she had a sense of humor. He'd never realized what a turn-on that could be. Sharing a few laughs with a woman made you want to get closer, to see what else you could share. It was almost as if they'd been friends for years, but had just never gotten around to meeting until now.

Or maybe his judgment wasn't as sound as he'd thought.

Yeah, well…he'd pretty well proved that, hadn't he?

By the time Marty heard Cole head downstairs in the middle of the day she had set out sandwich makings, a pitcher of iced tea and a pot of freshly made coffee. So far as she knew, he hadn't brought anything with him for lunch. If he took time out to drive to the Hamburger Shanty, it would just put her that much more behind schedule. During the hours when she had him, she wanted *all* of him.

The thought had wings. Before she could turn off her imagination, a mental image began to take shape. She groaned. There was *definitely* something missing in her life.

Passing him in the hall, she avoided looking directly at him, still miffed at being invited to stay out of his way. "Lunch is on the table. If it won't upset you too much, I'll just run upstairs and do some cleaning while you eat." Okay, call her a neat freak. At least it gave her the excuse she needed not to sit across the table and stare at that sexy mouth, those enigmatic eyes.

He said, "Look, I'm sorry if I was a little abrupt, okay? I didn't mean to offend you."

"Abrupt? Not at all," she dismissed. "You made your position perfectly clear, and believe me, I understand. If I let every part-timer I ever hired start telling me how to run things, I'd be out of business by now." Well, she was, wasn't she? "You know what I mean," she muttered.

Upstairs, her irritation evaporated as she took in the wreckage. The exposed skeleton of a wall and the dust and debris that coated every surface. *Clean it up, clean it up quick before someone sees it!*

And just like that, she was a kid again, trying her best to be perfect, hoping against hope that someone would like her enough to adopt her so that she could quit trying to be on her best behavior every minute of every single day, year after year after year. Surely somewhere there was a kind, loving couple who would notice how neatly she kept her few belongings and how perfectly she made her bed every morning. Someone who would recognize that underneath her gawky, homely disguise there was a little girl who was smart, pretty and obedient, who would make them a perfect daughter.

She blinked twice and she was back to the reality of the mess that had, until a few hours ago, been her neat upstairs hall. She'd been so busy looking beyond this particular stage to the result that she'd failed to consider what happened between the Before and the After.

Okay, so now she would deal with Between.

Peeling a trash bag from the roll, she began picking up the big pieces and wondering whether to sweep or vacuum the rest. Was it safe to plug her vacuum cleaner into the wall socket? There were wires showing between the studs or rafters or whatever those two-by-fours were called.

So much for her pretty yellow walls. Once there'd been an elegant little parquet table and an arrangement of pictures on the wall. The table had long since disappeared. Beau had given it to her the first year they were married, bragging that it was just a small part of his heritage. The only time he'd taken her to his home outside Culpepper, her reception had been cool to the point of intimidation. On the way back to Muddy Landing he'd explained everything she'd seen—the house, every stick of furniture, plus all the paintings—were family heirlooms. It went without saying that anything that came from the Owens family couldn't be considered joint property, even if he'd given it to her as a birthday or Christmas gift.

At least her first husband had given her a home. Alan had signed the deed over to her shortly after they were married, almost as if he'd known he had only a few more years to live. She would like to think she'd risen to the challenge of juggling a full-time job with a full-time marriage, because even before he'd been diagnosed with MS, Alan had required considerably more energy than her first book-store. Not because he'd been particularly demanding, but because she'd been so anxious to be the perfect wife.

But then he'd fallen ill and she'd spent the next few years on automatic pilot. With the bills piling up, she hadn't been able to afford to close down. Instead, she'd hired someone to mind the store while she'd stayed home with Alan.

After he died, she had forced herself to set her grief aside and resurrect what was left of her business. Gradually over the next few years, she had started breaking even, slowly moving into the black—but then the recession had hit. Her landlord had raised her rent, claiming increased property taxes, and by that time the online booksellers had started selling used as well as new. The rest, as they say, was history.

Now, unless this plan of hers worked out, she might as well go back to square one. As tired as she was, both men-tally and physically, she might not make it to square two.

With renewed resolve, she plugged in the vacuum cleaner and, when nothing blew up, picked up the wand and promptly knocked over three short two-by-fours. "Well, crud!"

From downstairs, Cole heard the Shop-Vac start up and stop. He heard something clatter to the floor, heard her ex-clamation and shook his head. Who *was* this woman he'd signed a contract with? He'd thought he had her pretty well sized up until he'd heard her talking about some guy's yacht, inviting the crew to some party and letting the games begin.

What games?

A few minutes later when they met on the stairs again, Cole stepped aside to allow her and her bulging sack of trash to pass. "I put the leftovers away," he said, amused at the belligerent set of her delicate jaw. Skin like thick cream…color and texture. He wondered idly what it would taste like. "Thanks for lunch. I didn't figure in meals when I made that estimate."

"No problem," she said airily. Dropping the sack at the foot of the stairs, she clutched her back.

"Got a problem?"

"Nope," she said brightly. "Not a one." Aside from the fact that she was freezing, having turned off the furnace earlier when she'd seen him prop the door open to bring in supplies.

She watched him lope up the stairs, his feet barely making a sound on the oak treads. Those shoulders were made for carrying stacks of lumber. As for his long, muscular legs…

Oh, shut up and get to work, Owens!

The phone rang again just as she opened the door to take the lumpy sack of trash outside. She paused, then decided whoever it was, she wasn't in the mood to talk.

"Want me to get that?" Cole called after the fifth ring.

Probably a telemarketer. "Suit yourself," she called back. Or it could be Sasha, wanting to talk about Faylene's new hot prospects down at the marina. As if she didn't have enough on her mind without getting involved in another matchmaking project. Personally, she'd rather indulge in a small panic attack, brought on by hiring a sexy itinerant carpenter to tear her house apart on a gamble that stood less than a fifty-fifty chance of paying off. A few quiet little screams, a minute or two of beating her head on the garage wall—that should get it out of her system.

In her more rational moments, which admittedly were few and far between these days, Marty was forced to conclude that reading was no longer a favorite pastime. Even for those who still read, there were too many competing sources for books. Flea markets and chain stores, thrift shops and libraries, not to mention the Internet. If only half of her old regulars bought two paperbacks a week from Marty's New and Used, that would mean…

"Oh, shoot," she muttered. Maybe she should have opened up a tattoo parlor.

The next time she saw her carpenter he was gray-haired. She couldn't think of anything she'd said or done to cause it. If he'd torn everything up only to change his mind about the job, she was miles up the creek without so much as a pair of water wings, much less a paddle.

She should have insisted on references. Just because Bob Ed had recommended him—just because he had Faylene's approval…

Oh, boy. To challenge or not to challenge. Only time would tell, but time was exactly what she didn't have.

She decided on the oblique approach. "Who was on the phone?" she asked, closing the front door behind her.

"It didn't say."

"*It?*"

He shrugged. "Must have been one of those 'If-a-guy-answers, hang-up' calls."

Oh, great. Now she was getting hang-up calls.

At four-thirty, when Marty bundled up to give Mutt his afternoon run, Cole was hauling out the last stack of broken plasterboard. "Dog walk?" he asked.

"Yep. Will you be here when I get back?"

When he glanced at his watch, she caught herself staring at the way the muscles in his forearm moved under a film of dust. "I'm at a good stopping place, but I'd like to get some material upstairs, ready to start putting up your new walls tomorrow."

Well, that sounded promising. She held the door open for him, then watched as he stacked the trash and covered it with a plastic tarp. There was something endearing about a man who took such pains with trash. Alan had left newspapers and clothing scattered throughout the house. Beau, after the first few months, hadn't stayed home long enough to litter.

Cole watched her tug on earmuffs and a pair of thick knit gloves. Her nose and cheeks were already reacting to the cold wind. A complexion like that—Scottish or Irish ancestry, most likely—was the next best thing to a lie detector. Not that he thought she'd lied to him, but after Paula he was conditioned to expect any woman to lie if the truth happened to be inconvenient. With Paula, lying had been a catch-me-if-you-can game.

After a while he hadn't bothered to try.

"Want me to lock up when I leave?" he called as she was about to climb into her minivan.

"Not unless you're worried about your tools." Without waiting for a reply, she backed out onto the street just as a gray Mercedes pulled out of a driveway three houses down the street. It waited for her to pass before heading in the same direction. He noticed the car only because it was a few decades old—a nicely restored classic, in fact. The truck he drove now was one of Bob Ed's rent-a-junkers, but he could definitely appreciate a fine piece of machinery.

Mutt was excited to see her. "I guess he's bored," she said to the part-time attendant, a kid with a blue Mohawk and a gold earring, while she struggled to attach the leash to the dog's choke collar. She felt a little embarrassed to be using the thing, but Annie had told her it didn't hurt him at all—it helped to slow him down when he saw something he wanted to chase.

"What he needs is a few trucks to run after," Blue Mohawk said cheerfully.

"Pity the poor truck if he ever caught one."

"Naw, he'd just water the tires. You seen all these big, tall trucks. Now you know how they got that way."

Marty rolled her eyes and led the dog out, nearly tripping over him when he tried to wrap himself around her knees.

"What you need, my dear Super-Mutt, is a crash course in manners," she panted once the big shaggy creature pulled her out to the path that served as a sidewalk. "Take a left! Left! That way, dammit!"

They went right, toward the Hamburger Shanty, where Mutt knocked over a trash container and then tried to tackle her when she bent to collect the blowing garbage.

A gray Mercedes cruised past as if looking for a parking place. There were several available, but evidently the driver didn't care for the specials posted in the window. Triple cheeseburger, double fries, thirty-six-ounce drink? What's not to like, as long as you've got the metabolism of a hummingbird.

Mutt was sniffing at Egbert Blalock's tan Buick. The bank had just closed, and evidently the new vice-president was picking up a take-out supper. Egbert was known to be as stingy with the bank's money as if it were his own— which probably wasn't a bad thing in a banker.

"You want to pee on his tires? Be my guest."

This time the dog obeyed, but she knew better than to take credit for it.

It was barely five-thirty when she got home again, but already it was practically dark. Her lower back was zapping her after trying to hang on to Mutt's leash with one hand while she picked up the garbage he'd spilled with the other. Those platter-size feet of his could probably topple a Dumpster. Fortunately, he hadn't tried.

She was dimly aware of the gray sedan turning the corner of Parliament and Sugar Lane behind her.

"Need a hand?" Cole's face, showing only concern, appeared at the driver's window.

He was still here. Was that a laugh line or a wrinkle in his left cheek? Disgusting how attractive lines in a man's face could be, when women were forced to spend a fortune on wrinkle removers.

She opened the door, but her feet were no longer responding to orders from headquarters. "No, thanks." And then, because he still looked dubious, she said, "Did you ever try wrestling five hundred pounds of untrained mongrel that's determined to sniff every weed along the path? On both sides of the street?" Not to mention pee on every blade of grass along the way. She sighed and managed to extract first one leg and then the other without actually grimacing.

"This is a daily thing? The dog-walking?"

"Twice daily. I'm doing a favor for friends who've been looking forward to this trip for ages. The boarding kennel wouldn't accept Mutt unless someone agreed to walk him at least twice a day, because he's too big for the short runs they provide."

Actually, Mutt's owners weren't really friends of hers. They lived a few blocks over, but Annie had once been a regular customer and they'd been desperate. And Marty had needed the money.

She limped toward the house while Cole deposited another bag of trash on the area he'd set aside. Food first, she promised herself—then a hot soak and bed. Those strong hands of his on her lower back wouldn't be unwelcome, either, she thought wistfully

Quit it! The last thing you need is another man in your life.

As he was right behind her all the way to the front door, she tried not to limp. Tried not to collapse, coat, earmuffs, gloves and all, on the living room sofa. Instead, she turned and asked, "Was there something you needed?"

"You had three more phone calls."

She lifted an eyebrow. At least she still had a few muscles that worked without causing pain. "Well?"

"A Ms. Beasley who said she could come any day next week if you want to start setting up the books. I think she's the one I met at the marina, who told me you needed a builder. You're to call her when you're ready."

Marty murmured, "Bless her heart." Faylene knew very well Marty was nowhere near ready for that.

Standing close enough so that she could smell a combination of freshly sawed lumber and a subtle aftershave, Cole continued. "There was a call from someone named Sasha. At least, that's what it sounded like. Anyway, she has some carpet samples she's bringing by in the morning."

"I'm not nearly ready for carpet and she knows it." More curiosity. "Anything else?"

"Another of those 'If-a-man-answers, hang-up' calls."

Marty closed her eyes. "Oh, shoot, shoot, shoot. I hate that kind of thing, don't you? It ought to be against the law."

"Probably just a wrong number."

When she opened her eyes again, he was still there. Still looking big and solid and protective and all the good things the romance stories described—things that she had never personally experienced. If she'd needed another clue that she was almost ready for an over-the-counter de-stress medication, that was it.

"Look, I closed up the house and turned on the heat again. Why don't you take off a few layers while I make you a pot of coffee? Once you warm up, maybe you'll feel more like—"

Better yet, turn the dog loose, call a cruise line and make reservations for two and you're on. What was it that caused two strangers to bond based on a few casual exchanges?

Or at least, caused one person to bond?

Five

Cole ended up staying for supper, partly because he had nothing better to do and partly because her house, even with a faint lingering odor of polyurethane and burnt cinnamon, was a hell of a lot more comfortable than the *Time Out* with its faint odor of mildew and inefficient space heater.

It has nothing to do with the woman, he assured himself. Nothing to do with the fact that he enjoyed her company—enjoyed even more speculating about what she'd be like in bed. So far as he could tell, she hadn't done a single thing to attract his attention.

Maybe that was it. She used natural bait, not an artificial lure.

He had no business fishing in these particular waters, no matter how tempted he was. On the other hand, she looked as if she needed someone to dump on. Her two friends probably had their own baggage. At least, she didn't seem too eager to speak to either of them.

He happened to be both handy and baggage free. A disinterested party, so to speak.

And you're going to damn well stay that way, right?

Right!

"The thing is," Marty said as she opened a diet drink and a bottle of Blackhook porter, "I really don't have time for fun and games right now." She handed him the ale. "Do you want a glass for that?"

"Bottle's fine." Fun and games? She'd explained briefly about their favorite pastime of matchmaking—which explained part of the conversation he'd overheard. "Don't your victims have anything to say about it?"

"I'd hardly call them victims. I mean, look how many people try to meet other people in chat rooms. And lots of people go on blind dates."

"Of their own free will. Nothing's forced on them."

"We've never forced anything on anyone," she protested. "All we do is arrange for X to meet Y, and they can take it from there."

"X and Y as in chromosomes?"

"Hadn't thought of it that way," she said, gray eyes twinkling. "Anyway, I'm too busy trying to figure out how to fit a bunch of ten-foot bookshelves into my two front rooms to worry about the social life of our neighborhood CPA. Any advice would be greatly appreciated."

"Your CPA's probably about to have all the social life she needs, with tax season looming dead ahead."

"I meant advice with the bookshelves."

"Oh. Right." What the hell, he wasn't one of her busy-buddies. What did he know about matchmaking? "That's not a problem."

"Maybe not in theory. Just whack the shelves in two and close up the open ends. I'm good at theory, just not so great when it comes to the actual whacking and closing."

"I can do one or two for you after supper."

Her doubtful look gradually gave way to a smile that was all the more effective for a tiny chip on the corner of a front tooth. Oh, man, this natural bait was wicked stuff.

"You don't have to do that," she protested.

He was tempted to agree. It wasn't a part of their agreement. On the other hand, he wasn't particularly eager to go back to the marina. This small yellow bungalow, even with a portion of the second floor gutted, was a hell of a lot more comfortable than the cold, damp cabin of a forty-year-old cruiser.

Yeah, sure. The house is the only attraction.

She was saying something about the dog, about how she was already dreading tomorrow's walk. "Rain or shine, he has to get out twice a day for a run, and the Hallets won't be back for... Oh, lawsy, five more days? I'm not sure my arms will survive."

Cole helped clear away the remains of supper as if he'd been doing it all his life. It had been Paula who'd insisted on hiring a combination cook-housekeeper. When he'd protested that with only the two of them they didn't really need it, and besides, they couldn't afford it, she had meekly agreed. A few weeks later he'd received a surprise promotion and a hefty raise.

He'd been excited at first about getting in on the architectural side of the business. That had always been his goal. He'd even managed to get half a degree in architecture before he'd damaged his left knee, putting an end to his football scholarship.

But not even when he'd been relegated to the job of selecting from a set number of styles and floor plans and making superficial changes among them had he tumbled to the fact that he was a kept man.

Once he'd been given the job of working on more challenging projects like the Murdock Office Complex and the Josephine Civic Center, he'd settled in and actually begun to enjoy the work.

That is, until too many accidents had aroused his suspicions and he'd started coming in early and staying late, poking into areas that were out of his jurisdiction.

Now he followed Marty into the living room, where she pointed out the potential placement of her bookshelves. "That wall's the longest. There are eleven of them, and if possible, I'd like to fit them into these two rooms." She waved a hand, indicating the small dining room that currently doubled as a home office. "I thought I'd use the kitchen for an office and box room. The table won't fit upstairs, but it'll be great for unpacking."

Stroking his stubbled jaw—he was a twice-a-day shaver when neatness counted—Cole studied the layout. One thing about living aboard a small boat—you learned to make the most of every square inch of space.

"Sasha has some wild ideas about colors—she's this friend I was telling you about. You spoke to her on the phone? Anyway, she's an interior designer—she's supposed to be tops in this area—but she thinks I need to paint my walls three different shades of red—can you believe it? She says with the north light I need to make it not just inviting, but exciting."

The room was already inviting, to Cole's way of thinking. Walls painted a warm, creamy shade with furnishings a comfortable mixture of old and not-quite-so-old. It looked just right to him. Nothing really outstanding—at least, nothing that screamed, "Keep off the furniture!"

Paula had insisted on an all-white color scheme to show off her art collection. He'd hated the damn stuff, her so-called art included.

Marty had a couple of pictures on the wall. One a reproduction of a marsh scene, the other a factory-produced oil of a cloudy sunset on the water. Both were pleasant enough. Hell of a lot better than Paula's primary color abstracts, anyway.

Walking around the two rooms that, along with the kitchen and a laundry-utility room, made up the first floor, Cole mentally transposed the bookshelves with the furniture that currently occupied the space. Damn shame to crowd all this into one room upstairs, but it was her house.

Marty was following him around like a hungry pup waiting for a handout. He was no miracle worker. He could remodel her second floor, but he couldn't guarantee anything beyond that. Sensing her anxiety, he said, "You've got choices, you know."

"Choices. You mean colors?"

He heard her sigh and turned to find her only a couple of steps behind. Too close. His hand brushed her hip and electricity sizzled. The way she jumped back, she must have felt it, too.

Sounding slightly breathless, she said, "I'll have to fight for them. Did you ever hear of a velvet-covered steamroller? That's Sasha."

"I'm talking about your arrangements, not your color

scheme." Her mouth looked soft, tired and discouraged. Staring at it, he thought, What the hell—a little encouragement wouldn't cost him anything.

Fortunately, before he could act on his impulse, his survival instinct kicked in. Taking a deep breath, he said, "You want to know what I think? I'm betting you can hold your own against any steamroller, velvet-covered or not."

It drew the ghost of a response. Not quite a smile, but at least those full, naked lips didn't look quite so discouraged. "Yes, well…you don't know Sasha."

Nor was he sure he wanted to meet her.

Marty shook her head. "I've tried arranging those darn shelves ever which-a-way on paper, but the proportions are all wrong for here. I had them custom built for my old place, but—" She shook her head again. "Am I crazy to even think of doing what I'm doing? Don't answer that—it's way, way too late." This time she actually chuckled.

It affected him in more ways than he cared to admit.

"People remodel all the time. In a house this age, it's probably overdue."

"Sure, to add a downstairs bath and maybe a room or two over the garage, but turning it into a retail outlet?"

He was tempted to pull her head down on his shoulder and tell her not to worry, that it was always darkest before the dawn, or some other meaningless fairy tale.

"Customers have to be able to move freely, you know? They're not going to browse in a room where they feel claustrophobic."

Moving to stand behind her, Cole placed one hand on her shoulder and used his other to gesture. "Eighteen feet, right? Fifteen of usable space between the door and the corner. How about we cut a few of your bookshelves down to about six feet, butt them up against the wall here, here and here." He indicated the area, his arm brushing against her shoulder. "That should give you plenty of clearance on the open end, and you can use the corner space beside the door for wall shelves."

"Cut them down?" Regardless of what she'd said earlier about whacking, she sounded as if he'd suggested cutting her legs off just above the ankles. Spinning around, she had to step back to keep from stumbling. He was that close. When he put out a hand to steady her, her eyes widened, sucking him into the cloud-gray depths.

Flowers. Even with the faint echoes of paint and burnt spice, he smelled flowers. There wasn't a damn thing blooming in her yard. It had to be the woman herself. No makeup, wild hair, clothes that could have come from any thrift shop—and she smelled like a tropical garden.

He leaned closer. She froze, a deer-in-the-headlights look in her eyes. *Don't do it, man—you're starting something you're in no position to finish.*

"Like we talked about before—shorten them," he said gruffly, stepping back to a safe distance.

Her cheeks flushed with color, she nodded slowly. "And I could use the short ends over here—and here." She gestured toward the space between windows and on either side. "And there's still the dining room."

She gradually lost the bemused look, if that's what it was. He was no expert when it came to reading a woman's expression, but she no longer looked wary. Actually, she looked almost excited, and an excited Marty Owens was a little too infectious for his peace of mind. He moved back and leaned against the door frame while she walked around, motioning with her hands, muttering to herself—soft little sounds she probably wasn't even aware of making.

And who'd have thought gray eyes could darken and sparkle that way? He wondered if that was how she'd look in bed, after—

"I'd better be getting back to the marina." It was one thing to hang around and help her plan her building project. It was another thing entirely to—

Yeah, well…forget about that. "I'd like to get here about seven tomorrow, if that's not too early." That way she'd be out walking her dog and he could start work without any enticing distractions.

Marty watched until Cole's truck disappeared, allowing her imagination free range. What was it about men and the way they dressed? Ninety-nine out of a hundred might as well be wearing baggy bib overalls for all the difference it made. She might even know and like them personally, but there was no chemistry. No *click.*

And then, along came that one out of a hundred—a thousand—wearing faded jeans and a plain black tee, and she immediately started wondering….

Be still, my heart.

A few minutes later she gathered her wandering wits and focused on her immediate problem. At least, one of her problems. She wandered around, studying the available space and jotting notes on the back of an envelope. If she used the utility room instead of the kitchen for—

That wouldn't work. No way was she going to squeeze a washer and drier into her upstairs hall, even after remodeling. The living room and dining room would provide enough display space, using the kitchen for—

The refrigerator. Oh, shoot. All she'd have room for in her new kitchenette would be one of those dorm-size models.

She could worry about that later. Meanwhile, just when it seemed as if her plan was not going to work, suddenly everything was falling into place, thanks to a sexy carpenter with shaggy hair, greeny gold eyes and a smile that could melt porcelain.

All of which was totally beside the point, she reminded herself forcefully.

Still, ever since she'd conceived the idea, she had thought she'd considered every possible way to fit eleven ten-foot-long bookshelves into the available space. And said sexy carpenter had given her the answer.

On Wednesday morning Marty was up long before daylight, wide awake for once, even though she'd stayed awake far into the night mentally arranging and rearranging her new showroom. The kennel didn't open until seven, which was when Cole was due.

She gulped down a glass of orange juice, winced as it hit her empty stomach, then bundled up and hurried outside, leaving the front door unlocked. The damp, cold northeast wind was still howling like a chorus of banshees. Occasionally they got a day when the temperature hit the seventies in January, but not this year.

Mutt loved the weather. There was probably some polar bear in him somewhere. With his shaggy coat streaming out behind him, he galloped off down Water Street toward his favorite destination, the Hamburger Shanty. Yelling at him was like yelling at a long-haired locomotive. She did it anyway. According to an article in one of the women's magazines Sasha was always bringing her with the pertinent pages turned down, yelling was a great stress-reliever.

Mutt ignored the shouts. If any of the few passersby heard her and wondered if she was stark raving bonkers, one look should clear up the mystery. The damn dog marched to a different drummer.

Or galloped to a different scent. Nary a signpost along the way went un-watered nor a weed un-sniffed between the kennel and his favorite buffet, the trash bins outside the Hamburger Shanty that weren't emptied until later that morning.

There were a few cars in the parking lot. Staff, mostly, as the place wouldn't open for another twenty minutes or so. A semi-familiar gray Mercedes cruised by slowly, probably looking for a place that served breakfast. It was the same one she'd seen yesterday—and come to think of it, hadn't the same car been parked in the Caseys' driveway?

A house sitter, maybe. The Caseys were in Florida, but they hadn't mentioned a sitter the last time Marty had spoken to Ruth Casey before they'd left.

"All right, I'm coming!" she yelled, as Mutt lunged at the stray cat that was nosing around in what he considered his private pantry.

Some twenty minutes later she finally closed the door to his unit at the kennel.

The blue-haired kid grinned at her. "Reg'lar handful, ain't he."

She shot him a dirty look. "You could've at least helped me get him out of his choke collar."

"Not in my job description. Hey, they don't pay me enough to wrestle critters like him."

"What *do* they pay you for?" First she had ruined her lower back on all those heavy bookshelves, and now her arms were in danger of being pulled from the sockets.

"Answer the phone. Take money. Make reservations."

"Don't strain yourself," she jeered.

When had she turned into such a shrew? Was that one of the symptoms of a shortage of vitamin S?

Cole was there by the time she got home, his truck pulled over to one side to make room for her minivan. He was a thoughtful man—she'd already discovered that about him. Whether or not he was a competent carpenter remained to be seen. He was good at tearing up. What else was he good at? she wondered before she could stop herself.

Don't ask. There are more important things in life than sex.

Oh, yeah? Name one.

"Hello, I'm home," she called, wincing as she wriggled out of her coat and dropped it on the hall bench. Later she might hang it in the closet, but first she had to collapse and catch her breath. Once she found the energy she might pop a couple of ibuprofen and rustle up something for breakfast. A spoonful of peanut butter would be quick and easy.

Hearing footsteps, she glanced up to see her carpenter loping down the stairs. In those faded jeans and a black shirt, he was almost too macho to be a male model except maybe in one of those sporting goods catalogs.

"G'morning," she greeted, offering him a tired smile.

"Looks like you just lost a marathon," he observed.

"Came in on the ragtag end, as usual. Believe me, it's not worth the money."

"You, uh…get paid?"

She nodded. "If I'd been introduced to that damn dog before the Hallets left town, never in this world would I have agreed to go near him."

"That bad, huh?" Cole said a moment later when he rejoined her in the hall.

Bless his heart, he'd gone directly to the kitchen and switched on the coffeepot she'd left all ready for when she got back. It occurred to her that no man had ever made coffee for her before—not even one of her husbands.

For some reason, that made her want to cry.

Allergies. It had to be allergies. "He not only outweighs me by a ton, he out-stubborns me by a mile," she said. "Don't laugh, it's not as easy as you might think." She grinned, but her heart wasn't in it.

He was standing. She was still seated. Lacking the energy to turn away, she was faced with a portion of male anatomy that was somewhat dusty but nonetheless impressive.

He said, "I thought this was a personal favor you were doing for friends. Didn't you know what he was like when you offered to walk him?"

"I told you, I'd never even seen him before I agreed. The way Annie talked about him having his own furniture and all, I knew he was a house pet. I guess I expected a poodle, or maybe a cocker spaniel. How many people keep a Clydesdale in their house?" She began flexing her shoulders and heard a disturbing crackling sound near the back of her neck.

"Annie?" Cole prompted as he hung her coat in the closet.

"She's one of my best customers. Actually, I only know her from the bookstore. They live several blocks over, but I've never even met her husband. Faylene says he's a lawyer. She said he'd just won his first case after practicing for nearly six years, which is why they decided to celebrate with this cruise."

"First case, huh?"

She sighed and closed her eyes. "According to Faylene, but that doesn't make it gospel. Anyhow, when Annie called and asked me if I could pick him up at the kennel and walk him twice a day, I said sure." Marty didn't bother to add that the money Annie had insisted on paying her was a large part of the inducement. Opening her eyes, she lifted her gaze to his tanned, weathered face. "You know what? I'll bet they asked everyone else they knew, but all their friends turned them down. Dumb me."

He was smiling at her again. Lordy, the man was too much! He said, "Chalk it up to a learning experience. Next time the guy wins a case and wants to take another vacation, don't be so quick to volunteer."

He moved closer. She felt him touch her shoulder, felt the firm pressure of his thumbs on the rock-hard muscles at the back of her neck. Tipping her head forward, she groaned.

"Don't worry, you couldn't pay me enough to—ahh!"

"This where it hurts, the trapezius?"

"Oh, yesss," she purred.

Cole eased her around so that he could use both hands. She was as tense as a ten-pound test line with a sixty-pound channel bass on the other end. Under three layers of clothing the skin was like warm satin. He sniffed. Flowers again. He wondered if her whole body smelled like that, or...

A final gurgle from the kitchen announced that the coffee was ready. "You want to stay here in the hall or hit the sofa?"

"I'd rather hit a bed or a hot bath," she admitted with a weak chuckle, "but I don't think I can make it up the stairs."

If that was a hint, he wasn't taking it. No way.

Unfortunately, his body had lost contact with his brain. "You had breakfast yet?"

"Just juice." She put a hand on the small of her back and stood.

Come to think if it, he'd seen her grab her back a time or two yesterday. "Hey, are you sure you're all right?"

"I'm fine. Nothing a few ibuprofen won't take care of."

"How many?" Cole had been that route, only in his case it had been a prescription painkiller after he'd been worked over by a couple of thugs hired by his ex-father-in-law. That was all ancient history, but he'd learned a few valuable lessons in the process. Never trust a guy whose neck is thicker than the width between his ears, especially if he calls your father-in-law Boss. And don't risk ruining your brain and your belly with anything more potent than beer, ale, or the occasional glass of Jack's finest.

"How are we doing upstairs?" she asked with a smile that didn't quite reach her eyes.

In other words, he interpreted, *Butt out of my personal business.*

"I'll start closing the end section today. By tomorrow I should be ready to start on your cabinets."

"I don't want anything fancy."

"Just sketch out precisely what you have in mind. We've got a little leeway but not a whole lot."

Did that mean she was allowed to join him upstairs while he worked? How about after hours?

How about concentrating on what's important, Marty reminded herself. While Cole headed for the kitchen, she wandered into the living room and eased herself down onto the sofa. Her stomach didn't exactly welcome the thought of coffee, but she needed something to start her engine.

"Lots of cream," she called out.

"Yes, ma'am."

A polite carpenter. With good hands. Slow, firm hands that knew exactly where to touch and how much pressure to apply, stopping just short of actual pain. Sasha would have a field day if she could tune in on her musings right now, Marty thought, amused.

The coffee was welcome, even if her stomach was pumping acid by the gallon. Weeks ago she'd gone online and checked out everything she could find about stress and the physical manifestations thereof. How to avoid it, or at least how to deal with it. The trouble was, she didn't have time for tai chi. As for yoga, which she used to enjoy, she would never even make it past the Sun Salutes.

Music was another recommendation. Daisy had given her a dreamy New Age CD, but the stuff only made her race her engines, waiting for the music to get to the point instead of rambling all over the scale.

Yelling seemed to be her only option. It was free and the side effects were probably minimal—but she needed something to yell at. She was far too inhibited to step outside and do the primal scream thing.

"I made you some toast."

She opened her eyes. Pavarotti with the frog in his throat was back. He was too good to be real.

"Do you really need that ibuprofen?" he asked.

She sighed. "I guess not." Pills couldn't cure a broken back. She needed the pain to tell her how bad off she was.

"When do you have to do the next dog run?"

"This afternoon. Anytime between two and six when the kennel closes."

"I'll go with you. I need to go by the hardware store anyway for cabinet materials. What breed did you say this dog was?"

"St. Bernard and Clydesdale mix. Maybe some polar bear. Annie said they got him from the pound when he was nothing but a little ol' fuzz ball. Ha!"

"So now he's a big ol' fuzz ball."

Cole switched on a lamp to offset the gray morning. Instead of heading back upstairs, he settled into her one man-size chair. Marty struggled to a semi-reclining position. She'd rather stay flat, but siphoning coffee through a rubber hose wasn't an option, so semi seemed advisable.

"What about—you know?" She nodded toward the ceiling.

"Like I said, I'm ahead of schedule. I allow for a couple of short breaks during the day. Now, tell me what kind of wood you want. It makes a difference in how you want them finished. Raw, painted, pickled or varnished."

"What would you suggest?"

They discussed styles, wood finishes and hardware. "I'll take you to pick that out after I get the things built."

"Oh, so I finally get to voice an opinion. Does that mean I can go upstairs while you're there, or do I have to wait until you leave and write down a work order."

"My, my—snide, aren't we?"

"Yes, we are," she snapped, and took another sip of coffee. Which he had made and served, she reminded herself. After he'd laid hands on her and taken away more of her pain than he probably knew. Taken her mind off it, anyway.

She yawned. Bad back, dream-filled sleep…

The last thing she remembered was feeling the cup eased from her fingers. Then something light and warm drifted down over her body. He didn't turn off the lamp, but tilted the shade so it wouldn't shine in her eyes.

"Don't leave without me this afternoon," he said quietly.

"Mmm," she murmured.

The classic gray Mercedes was gone from the Caseys' driveway by the time they left home just before four that afternoon, Marty noticed. She tried to remember exactly when the Caseys had left. According to Faylene, who knew practically everyone in town and most of their business, they'd gone to Tampa to see their first grandchild. A boy. Named Todd.

"Weather's moderating," Cole observed.

They were in his rattletrap of a truck so he could pick up the lumber needed to do her cabinets and the book-shelves on the way home from walking Mutt.

Or rather, from chasing after the creature, trying to hang on to his lead. For once, Marty thought, relieved, she could trot along behind and let someone else do the hard work. Cole had even offered to go in and fetch the dog from his wire-walled cubicle.

"Be my guest," Marty said, leaning back against the headrest. Through sleepy eyes, she watched his hand on the gearshift. Nice hands…strong, but sensitive. She knew how they felt.

She yawned for the third time since they'd left home.

"Need another nap? What's the matter, does all the mess upstairs keep you from sleeping?" he asked.

Well…maybe his hands weren't what impressed her most, but they impressed her a whole lot.

"I sleep perfectly well," she lied. "It's this weather. Maybe I'm part bear. Cold, rainy days I tend to want to hibernate."

Did bears hibernate two to a cave? Maybe they were onto something, she mused.

A few minutes later when Cole and Mutt emerged from the door at the top of five wooden steps, Marty climbed out and joined them. Mutt was in high fettle. They reached the corner of Water and Third streets and Cole tugged lightly on the lead and flipped his right hand.

Mutt obediently veered right.

Marty stopped dead in her tracks. "How did you do that?"

"How did I do what?"

He was hatless. With the wind ruffling his hair and plastering his leather bomber jacket to his chest, he looked wildly attractive and more than a little dangerous.

"How'd you get him to turn there? I always have to pull my arms out of the sockets getting him to go where I want him to go."

"Don't you use hand signals?"

"Both my hands are occupied. In case you hadn't noticed, he pulls like a six-mule team."

"Marty, you do know he's deaf, don't you? Didn't they even tell you that much?" Cole snapped his fingers. The dog didn't even look around.

She shook her head slowly. She was beginning to believe there was a lot the Hallets hadn't told her—probably knowing that if they had, she might have refused the job.

"He's also got a ripe cataract in one eye."

"Well…shoot."

Mutt sat on his broad haunches, a big, sappy grin on his tricolored face, while Cole explained about his handicaps. "He's still got good vision in one eye. As for his hearing, all you have to do is see how he responds to hand signals."

"But—but I never gave him any hand signals," she protested.

"Not intentionally. He's obviously used to watching for them, though, so when you wave your hands first one way and then another, he's confused. Being a dog, he simply does whatever he wants to do, which is usually to mark his territory and explore any interesting scents."

Chagrined, Marty was still thinking about how many clues she had missed by the time they headed back to the kennel. She'd never owned a dog. Had always wanted one, but first there was school and then there was Alan to look after, and later she'd been too busy all day with Marty's New and Used. It wouldn't have been fair to leave a dog at home alone all day.

Excuses, excuses. The truth was, it took just about all her energy to manage her business without having to worry about looking after a pet.

Some women did it all, some didn't. She'd even managed to kill off a potted philodendron, which, according to Sasha, was all but impossible.

Mutt acted as though he was glad to be back, standing still—or as still as a big dog could when his stub of a tail was flapping a hundred miles an hour.

Cole went through a few basic signals and the big, shaggy dog performed beautifully, after which Mutt was rewarded with a bit of roughhouse tussling before he was shut into his compartment.

Leaving the building, Marty said, "You must have owned dogs, you know so much about them."

But before he could tell her how he'd come by his knowledge, a now-familiar gray sedan cruised past slowly.

Marty stopped, one hand on Cole's sleeve. "You see that car that just passed? If I didn't know better I'd think it was following me. Lately I seem to see it everywhere I go."

Cole watched as the 220SL disappeared around a corner, then he opened her door of his pickup. "They're not all that uncommon, even the older ones," he observed.

"I know that."

"If you didn't recognize it, it's probably an out-of-town visitor."

"This time of year? Any visitors we get in the wintertime are usually hunters, and they rarely drive Mercedes, not even the SUVs. Besides, I've seen this same gray car parked down the street in a neighbor's driveway, and I happen to know they're in Florida."

Six

Marty insisted on going to the lumberyard with him, and Cole indulged her. It was her money, after all. She was still chafing over the dog—over missing such obvious clues. If he hadn't known it before, he did now—she liked to be the one in control.

Most women did. Paula had disguised that side of her nature with a helpless, clinging-vine act that had held up for almost a year after they were married. Helpless like one of those pretty flowering vines that could conquer anything in its path, given enough time.

"Here y' go, sir. That be cash or credit?"

"Credit card," Marty said, pushing her gold card across the desk. "Might as well earn the three cents interest on my money between now and the end of the month."

"Pick up around back," the clerk said, and Marty marched ahead to lead the way through the vast metal building.

Strolling along behind her, Cole deliberately shortened his stride to let her go first. Funny woman. Militantly independent, smart enough to know when to shut up and listen, yet unafraid to admit when she was out of her depth. The way she had watched, listened and learned when he'd demonstrated how to control that big goofy dog was a good example. You had to admire a woman like that.

Somewhat to his surprise, Cole realized that he not only admired her, he liked her.

He loaded the lumber into the back of the truck, secured it with ropes from the toolbox on back, and turned back to where Marty waited. "If you don't mind my working late to make up the time, I'll go with you again in the morning to make sure you can handle him. Trouble with a deaf dog is that once he gets away from you, calling and whistling won't get him back."

"Believe me, I thought of that," Marty said grimly.

Before he could help her up, she grabbed the door frame and swung herself up into the cab.

He closed the door. "You'll do fine, but it won't hurt to be doubly careful."

Once they got back to the house she insisted on helping him unload the truck. "I can carry one end of the boards while you carry the other."

"Be easier if I balance 'em on my shoulder."

She looked at the two-by-fours and the yellow pine boards, then looked at his shoulder. They did it his way, which was far more efficient than having to juggle each plank between them. She went ahead to open the doors, and he watched her simply because she was worth watching, even in a down-filled coat, with her windblown hair tangling around her earmuffs.

By the time the last plank was stacked in the hallway upstairs it was almost dark. Marty insisted he stay for supper.

"It's the least I can do after you taught me dog language. It'll be something quick and easy. I'll just pop a couple of frozen dinners into the microwave."

Bad move, Cole told himself. Really bad move. After three days he was already having trouble thinking of her as just another employer. "You don't have to do this. I can stop off on the way to the marina and get take-out." In fact, he'd sort of counted on it. Meat, bread and two vegetables. Barbecue, hush puppies, slaw and fries. He knew how to take care of himself—had been doing it for nearly forty years now.

He followed her into the kitchen. It was a nice room. It reminded him of his mother's kitchen, only there was no sheet music scattered over every surface. Paula's kitchen had looked more like a laboratory—not that she'd ever spent much time in it. It occurred to him that he'd never thought of it as their kitchen, not even when they'd first moved in a few months after they were married. Her father had insisted on giving them the house, which had prompted Paula's one and only attempt at humor. She'd told him not to look a gift house in the mouth.

Marty left the utility door open while she checked out the contents of a small, chest-type freezer. With her jeans stretched tightly over her rounded behind, she leaned over to scramble through the contents. Cole made himself look away. Against the taut denim he could see the faint outline of her underpants. Definitely not a thong.

Cut it out, Stevens!

So he forced himself to check out his employer's kitchen instead of her personal assets, pretending a great interest in the double-hung windows over the sink, the leafy vine trailing down from a jar on the narrow sill and the sun-catcher hanging from the curtain rod. The yellow-and-white checked curtains matched the tablecloth. She went in for a lot of yellow. On a day like this, with barely enough daylight to wedge in an eight-hour day, it made the room feel warm and cheerful.

"Here we go," Marty announced, holding out two boxes, one a well-known diet brand, the other Salisbury steak with a side of macaroni and cheese. "Your choice."

He appeared to study the two flat boxes before choosing the two-hundred-and-eighty calorie delight.

She looked surprised. "Are you sure?"

Sure he was sure. It would serve as an appetizer until he could stop for his usual barbecue plate on the way to the marina. Odds were she was in for the night, and he didn't want her going to bed hungry.

They didn't talk much over supper. He studied the three tablespoonfuls of whatever it was he was eating and hoped his belly wouldn't embarrass him by protesting too loudly.

A few minutes later Marty shoved her plastic tray aside. "As Faylene would say, it's pretty good, what there is of it, and there's plenty of it, such as it is. You said you'd met her—Faylene Beasley? Bob Ed's friend? That's the way she talks most of the time."

"In circles, you mean," Cole said as he tried to remember what the woman had said about her friend who needed a small remodeling job done. "Look, about tonight—I said I'd work overtime to make up for taking off early, so—"

"You didn't take off early. You were still—that is—"

"Still on the clock?" he suggested, amused because she looked so embarrassed. He knew better than most that knocking down the barriers between employee and employer was asking for trouble.

"In a manner of speaking," she said primly, and he had to laugh.

To hell with the barriers.

And then she laughed, too. He lapped it up like a cat with a saucer of cream—the way her eyes kindled, the way her lips twitched at the corners just before she gave in and laughed aloud. He had a strong feeling that she hadn't done too much of that lately—laughing, that is. He didn't know why it bothered him, but it did.

When she stood and reached across the table for his tray and coffee mug, her hair swung over her shoulders, and he caught a whiff of that mysterious fragrance again. Flowers. Something soft, subtle and sweet—maybe shampoo, maybe hand lotion. Odds were she hadn't bothered to douse herself with perfume just for his benefit.

Jeez, he'd known her all of what—three days? A smart man would get the hell out before he did anything crazy, like touching her. Like seeing if all that rich mahogany hair of hers was as soft as it looked. Granted, he'd been through a long, dry spell—he was probably suffering from a buildup of testosterone. But there was nothing wrong with his brain. He *knew* what he ought to do.

The hard part was doing it.

"Tell you what," he announced, sliding his chair away from the table and glancing down to make sure he could pass muster without pulling his shirttail out of his jeans. "I'll measure up one of your bookshelves and cut the end boards and braces before I leave. First thing tomorrow we can finish it up. Then, while I work upstairs, you can decide if you want the rest of them cut down the same way. What do you say?"

She said yes.

They worked in the garage, with barely enough room to move around. The only way he could keep from brushing against her was to work on the opposite side of the project, but even that didn't prevent contact. As the garage wasn't insulated, Marty had bundled up in an old coat and pulled a stocking cap down over her ears. She should have looked like a ragamuffin kid. Instead, she looked—

Yeah, well…let's not go there, Cole warned himself.

"That ought to do it," he said after the final cut had been made and the short section laid aside. He stood, flexed his back and looked around for a broom.

"Don't bother, I'll clean up in the morning," she told him. "Would you like—that is, the coffee's still warm."

And so was he. Warm didn't begin to describe the way he was feeling after spending the past half hour working in a small crowded space, brushing hands and shoulders, even backing into her a few times. Purely accidental touches, but that didn't make it any easier to ignore the electricity that sparked between them.

He wondered if she'd even noticed, and decided she hadn't. Otherwise, she'd never have invited him to stay for coffee.

"I'd better get on back to the marina and run the bilge pump before I turn in." Yeah, that'd do it, all right. Cram his six feet two inches and one-hundred-eighty-seven pounds into a shower a quarter of the size of a phone booth while he rinsed off the sawdust, and then try to get to sleep on a bunk designed for a guy half his age and half his size.

It occurred to him that the lifestyle that had seemed so great back when he'd first decided not to look for an apartment in the Norfolk area wasn't turning out quite the way he'd planned.

Hell, now he even wanted to get himself a dog.

The first day of February produced a few adventurous crocuses and the promise of an early spring. Marty had slept like a log—dreamed a lot of crazy stuff that left her tingling and vaguely unsatisfied when she first opened her eyes, but the dreams quickly faded as she stood zombie-like under the shower.

Walk the dog. Had Cole said to wait for him? She couldn't remember, but even if he had, she didn't recall agreeing. Better if he started putting her amputated book-shelf back together while she put Mutt through his paces.

Hand signals. Surely she could remember the ones he'd showed her yesterday. Right, left, stop, sit, stay. What else? Quit peeing on the dandelions? Leave that poor cat alone?

She saw headlights flash across the front window be-fore she'd even gotten the coffeepot ready for when she got back. Darn it, she needed to do this by herself, if only to prove that she could.

But it was Sasha's red convertible, not Cole's pickup truck that pulled up behind her minivan. Curbing her im-patience, she opened the front door. "Isn't this a bit early, even for you?" Contrary to appearances, her glamorous friend started her working days early and sometimes worked into the wee hours.

"Give me a doughnut and tell me how he's working out," Sasha demanded.

"They're in the freezer. You'll break a tooth. How who's working out?" As if she didn't know. Where bachelors were concerned, Sasha's radar system was the envy of governmental agencies all over the world.

The interior designer stamped the damp earth off her three-hundred-dollar stiletto-heel shoes, then brushed past Marty and headed for the kitchen in a cloud of her favorite Odalisque. "Open your eyes, take a deep breath and wake up, hon."

"Don't you have anything to eat at your house?" Marty grumbled. Sasha knew she was never at her best this time of morning. Today was even worse than usual, thanks to spending half the night dreaming dreams that refused to disperse.

"Why bother? I'm always out for lunch and dinner, and you're right on my way for breakfast." Sasha plopped her well-rounded behind in one of the mule-eared kitchen chairs. "So tell me this—have y'all been to bed yet?"

Marty was tempted to say yes. Technically, it was no lie. She'd been to bed and she assumed Cole had, too—only not together. "Sash, he's my carpenter. That's *all* he is, okay?"

"Just asking. I still want him for Lily. Faye says he's perfect, but if you're interested, I guess we can find somebody else for her."

"I am not interested!" Marty all but shouted. "At least not that way. But if you distract him so he can't finish up my work on time, I'll never forgive you."

"Pish-tush. Course you will, honey. Besides, all we want for Lily is whatever's left after you get through with him."

"Argh," Marty growled.

"Did I tell you I'm doing this place on the bay for the CEO of PGP? Hey, if you don't have Krispy Kremes, how about some cinnamon toast? Lots of butter, lots of sugar, just a dash of cinnamon?"

"Sorry, I burned up all my cinnamon. Plain buttered whole wheat is the best I can do."

"Oh, God, you're just so disgustingly wholesome. Is that him? I heard a truck out front."

Well, shoot. "You hung around deliberately just so I'd have to introduce you, didn't you."

The redhead's smug look was all the answer Marty needed. By that time Cole was at the door and there was nothing she could do to postpone the inevitable.

"You ready to roll?" he called as he stepped into the hall.

"Come on in the kitchen a minute. There's someone I want you to meet." Sure, she did. Like she wanted a face full of zits.

"Sasha, this is Cole Stevens. Cole, Sasha." Through narrowed eyes, she watched for any reaction.

Cole grinned and looked over the short, shapely, over-dressed redhead without even bothering to disguise his interest. Amazement or amusement, she couldn't be sure.

"Nice to meet you, Ms. uh—Sasha. I believe we spoke on the phone."

Sasha all but drooled. "Well, my goodness gracious, aren't you a sight for sore eyes." It was a statement, not a question.

"Sasha," Marty warned softly.

"I just meant, poor Marty's been so desperate for a man—that is, for someone to tear her house up and put it back together again."

"Oops, look at the time. I guess you'll have to stop off at IHOP on the way north," Marty said with a grim smile. Sasha didn't have a mean bone in her body, but mischief was her middle name. "Cole's got work to do, I've got to walk Mutt, and then we've got loads of stuff to accomplish today— Isn't that right, Cole?"

He nodded obediently, those tarnished brass eyes gleaming with amusement. She would have swatted him if it wouldn't have given Sasha so much satisfaction. Nothing the redhead liked better than stirring up a hornet's nest.

"Nice meeting you, ma'am."

"Oh, would you just listen to that. Isn't he sweet?"

"Sasha…"

"Have you thought any more about those colors I showed you?" she asked as Marty urged her toward the front door. "With that big north-facing window—"

"I'm giving it a lot of thought," Marty lied as she all but pushed her friend out the door. And then listened to the throaty chuckles that drifted in her wake like a cloud of her favorite perfume. "With friends like that," she muttered, "who needs enemies?"

"Is she, uh, in show business?" Cole asked when she rejoined him in the kitchen.

"You mean just because she's wearing a red leather skirt, a yellow fur jacket and chandelier earrings, not to mention white lace stockings and those five-inch heels? I think it's the Napoleon complex. She doesn't want to risk being overlooked."

Cole shook his head slowly as he led her out to the truck. "Not much chance of that," he said. "I didn't catch her last name. Does she have one?"

"She has at least five—one of her own and four ex-husbands to pick from. I never know which one she's using, so I usually don't bother to use one."

"Madonna. Cher. Sometimes one name's enough."

"I hadn't thought of it that way, but that's probably it."

Evidently done with the subject of her friend's various

names, he said, "I figure we can put Mutt through his paces and be back by eight, unless you have stops to make."

She didn't. And this wasn't the way she'd planned for the morning to go, but she surrendered to the inevitable. Less trouble that way.

She really should have insisted on taking her car, though, because his truck was a little too cozy. The scent of leather, soap and coffee from the mug in the cup-holder teased her senses. That was before he switched on the engine and the strains of classical piano poured from the speaker.

Classical piano? Had he made a mistake and turned on WUNC, the closest PBS station?

Halfway to the kennel, the music was still playing. She recognized it vaguely as Chopin, but couldn't have named it if her life depended on it. While they waited for one of Muddy Landing's three streetlights—the last two were new, and they hadn't quite got the timing down yet—he whistled softly under his breath, following the melody perfectly.

"You want me to take him?" he asked.

"No, thanks. I can do it now that I know what the problem is."

"Fine," he said cheerfully. "I'll just stick around in case he gets distracted by that cat again. Like I said, if he gets away—"

"I know," she cut in. "Call nine-one-one and get someone to sound the tornado warning."

She knew what to do about the dog. What she didn't know was what to think of a man who drove a truck that had to be at least ten years old and was showing signs of rust. A man who lived on a boat and whistled Chopin.

A man who barged into her private dreams as if he had

every right to be there, leaving her all hot and bothered. If she couldn't manage that damn dog, it would be his fault, not hers, Marty thought rancorously.

In fact, Mutt was on his best behavior. Thanks to the hand signals, he actually allowed her to fasten on his choke collar without stepping on her feet more than a couple of times. Of course he whacked her with his stub of a tail and slobbered on her hand, but, as Cole said, that was only because he liked her.

She hated to think of the damage the creature could do if he didn't.

They'd gone only a few hundred feet down Water Street when the gray Mercedes pulled away from the curb and crept forward.

Cole touched her shoulder and said quietly, "Keep going. I'll catch up with you."

Before she could ask what he was going to do, he wheeled around and jogged back along the weedy path. Turning to stare after him, Marty was nearly pulled off her feet until she remembered the hand signal that meant Be still, you big lug.

Just as Cole got to within twenty-five feet of the car, the driver hooked a left and took off down Third Street. Cole stared after it for several moments before returning to where Marty and Mutt waited.

He said, "Damnedest thing," and shook his head.

"Then you don't think I'm crazy? He really is following me?"

"If so, it's about the worst job of covert action I've ever seen. Not that I've seen all that many, but still…"

"What do you think he wants?"

"What do you have?"

While she was trying to come up with some reason why a stranger would be keeping tabs on her, Cole took over Mutt's lead. He allowed the dog to explore the river's edge instead of continuing to the end of the run, which was usually the Hamburger Shanty.

"I'm just guessing, but if he was looking for something in your possession, he'd wait for you to leave and then search your house." They were facing east. The sun was low enough so that he had to squint, lending him a dangerous look. "You'll have to admit, you make it easy for him."

Marty nodded slowly. "I'm beginning to feel like I'm trapped in the middle of a suspense plot."

"A what?"

"Plot. Books. You know—whodunnit, to whom did they do it, and why? Don't you read fiction?"

"Sure—Cussler, Patterson, guys like that. I see what you mean, though."

Marty made up her mind on the spot to introduce him to a few female authors. Men were good—some a lot better than good—but there was a certain subtlety in woman's suspense that was addictive.

"Well, anyway, I don't have anything worth stealing, and like you say, even if I did, why would he keep following me instead of searching my house? It's not like I ever lock the door."

"But you will from now on, right?"

"Definitely." For the time being, anyway. Until she figured out what this stalking business was all about. Probably a mistake.

"So if it's nothing you have in your possession, what do you know that someone might be interested in?"

"You mean like that famous Senate hearing? What did

he know and when did he know it? Beats me. Maybe he's a headhunter. Waldenbooks wants to hire me to open up a Muddy Landing branch."

Cole took her arm as they headed back to the kennel, a grinning, tail-waving Mutt leading the way. "Until we know better, though, the next time—"

Marty finished it for him. "Right. Next time he comes after me I'll march right up to him and demand to know what the dickens is going on. How much are they offering? Is it going to be a stand-alone store or just a cubbyhole in the mall? Not that we even have a mall, unless you count Dinky's Ice Cream Parlor with the drivers' license place on one side and Paul's Hair Salon on the other."

Cole chuckled, and the sound shivered down Marty's spine, reminding her of those torrid dreams. Reminding her that certain areas in her life had been too long neglected. She said, "Maybe I'll do it while I still have Mutt. That ought to scare the truth out of him."

"I was thinking more like taking Mutt home with you, just in case your stalker decides to drop by. I can run any errands you need so you won't have to go out. If he gets desperate enough, we might be able to force his hand."

Marty halted. Mutt didn't. When she regained her balance, she said, "Hold on. Wait just a cotton-pickin' minute here. If you think I'm letting this hairy elephant inside my house, you're crazy. Things are in a big enough mess without that."

"Yeah, and he'd still need walking." Cole went on as if she hadn't even spoken. "I can take care of that, but that would leave you home alone." He led the way up the kennel steps and took over the unhitching before turning Mutt into his compartment.

Marty waited to respond until he'd hung up the leash and collar. "Actually, I've been thinking about getting a dog now that I won't have to go off and leave him alone all day. Nothing over fifty pounds, though. Smaller would be even better. A Jack Russell, maybe. Or a beagle—even something from the pound, as long as it's small."

She called a greeting to the blue-haired kid who was reading a comic book behind the counter. Once they reached the three-car parking lot she automatically scanned the street in both directions. Two trucks, a delivery van and a rusty Camaro passed by. Marty waved to the woman driving the Camaro.

"Sadie Glover. She works at the ice-cream place. She was one of our, um…projects last fall."

"Projects?"

"Don't ask." Usually it didn't bother her—talking about their matchmaking. Everybody knew what was going on, and nobody really minded. At least, nobody ever said so—except for Faylene, after their botched attempt to pair her up with Gus Mathias before they'd found out she'd already been seeing Bob Ed.

"Look, I still don't like leaving you home alone at night," Cole said as he assisted her into his high cab. "Fasten your seat belt."

She did. "I thought we agreed that whoever it is, he's not after me personally. If that was the case, he could've caught me long before now. It's not like I've been hiding."

Cole walked around the front and got in. "That's what's so puzzling," he said thoughtfully as he pulled out of the parking lot onto the street. "He parks near your house, right?"

She nodded. "In the Caseys' driveway."

"He follows you when you leave, but he hasn't tried to break in and he hasn't approached you. Something doesn't add up."

"Maybe he thinks he knows me, but he's not sure. You know, like maybe we were classmates or something?"

"Possible, I guess."

"Or you know what I think? He's waiting for me to lead him to something. Or someone. The question is, who or what?" She had to laugh. "I guess as detectives, neither of us is ready for prime time, huh?"

He chuckled along with her, and Marty thought how comfortable it was, being able to trust a man enough to laugh with him—to have him worry with her and about her.

Although *comfortable* wasn't quite the word she would have used to describe the sensation that shot through her when they pulled into the driveway and he came around to help her down. She wasn't used to being helped, even from a seat that was four feet off the ground.

She had the door open and was feeling around with her heel to find the narrow chrome bar that served as a step down when he caught her in his arms. He didn't set her down right away.

Laughing breathlessly, she said, "Didn't they used to call those things running boards back in the Dark Ages? And weren't they a lot bigger?"

And then her laughter faded, and so did his. Her breath snagged somewhere in the middle of her chest as his face went out of focus. At the last instant, she closed her eyes.

A voice that echoed none of the panic she was feeling whispered that she didn't even know this man. Yet she knew him in the most elemental sense, as if she'd known him all her life only not in this guise.

Then it was too late to think, as senses too long deprived burst into life. She felt the soft, moist brush of his lips on hers. No pressure, no demands, just…touching.

As the kiss slowly deepened, it was as if she'd been asleep for a hundred years and had woken up in a brand-new world to the tantalizing taste of mint laced with coffee. To the scent of bath soap and leather and sun-warmed male skin. To the iron-hard arms that held her breathlessly close—all elements combined to stoke a powerful hunger that demanded fulfillment.

He did a thorough job of it, she thought fleetingly as his tongue explored her mouth. His lips lifted to brush kisses on her eyelids, her temples, and then returned to the starting place.

Her carpenter. Her kissing carpenter, her upstairs man. Her bodyguard and dog walker and problem solver.

"Well," she breathed. Once he finally lifted his face and she found enough air to speak, she couldn't think of another thing to say. "Well…"

"Got that out of the way."

She noticed that he sounded just a tad shaken, too.

"You want to fire me? Go ahead, I'll understand."

She shook her head. Fire him? No way. Things might be infinitely more complicated after this, but if he walked away now she'd probably chase after him, begging him to come back.

"Got what out of the way?" she asked breathlessly.

"You telling me you haven't thought about what it would be like? Kissing?"

She'd never been any good at lying, so she said nothing.

Seven

With her synapses firing off like Fourth of July fireworks as they entered the house, Marty couldn't organize a single coherent thought. No other man had affected her the way this one did.

At least not since she was fifteen and was exposed to a sullen sixteen-year-old dropout who knew dirty words that hadn't even been invented, who could swear in two languages, had a world-class sneer and carried a pack of Camels in the rolled-up sleeve of his T-shirt. James Dean redux.

"You do the—the—you know—the bookcases," she said, tugging off her stocking cap and massaging her scalp as if it might encourage circulation to her brain. "I need to—to—um…"

Cole nodded as if she'd made herself perfectly clear. If he was suffering any of the same aftereffects, he hid it well. "I'm headed to the hardware store. I shouldn't be gone more than half an hour or so, but I want you to lock up behind me, all right? Don't open the door to anyone until I get back unless you've known them for at least five years."

"Does that include you?" Okay, so she had a few of her wits together now. "Aren't we being a wee bit paranoid?"

A watery streak of sunlight slanted in through a west-facing window, turning his eyes to pure jade. It occurred to her that his hair didn't look quite so shaggy today. Either he'd had a trim or she was getting used to his brand of casual.

"Paranoid? Let's hope so. If we're making too big a deal of it, there's no harm done, but just in case…"

"In case the Muddy Landing Mafia is after a fortune in used first-edition paperbacks, you mean? I promise, at the first sign of imminent attack, I'll call the FBI."

With a quick twitch of his lips, he said solemnly, "Repeat after me, 'I will lock the door. I will not let any strangers inside until Cole gets back.'"

Marty, who had never been given to theatrics, threw out her hands and rolled her eyes. "All right, all right! What is *happening* to my nice, dull, orderly life?" She held up one finger. "I wake up one morning and some creep is stalking me." Held up another one. "My house is falling down around my ears." Third finger. "I'm ordered to lock my door in case the bogeyman tries to get in." All five fingers on both hands.

"Hey," he said softly, capturing her hands and folding them into his own. "It's not as bad as it looks. We big-city guys just tend to be a little more cautious, so humor me, will you?"

She nodded. Didn't even try to speak because she'd probably throw herself in his arms and beg him not to leave her. He was still holding her hands as if he'd forgotten to release them, so she did it for him. Pulled away while she still could. If she'd needed a reminder that too much stress could be hazardous to a woman's health there was no need to look any further for the cause. One kiss from a man who reminded her of all the good things a man could be, but rarely was, and she was trying to twist her uneventful life into a plot for a romantic suspense.

His quick kiss missed whatever he'd been aiming for and slid off the side of her nose.

A moment later Marty watched him lope across the front yard, open the truck door and swing himself up into the high cab.

"You Tarzan, me Jane," she whispered. "Ya-hoo!" It was more rebel yell than jungle cry. She couldn't even get that much right.

In the kitchen, she opened the refrigerator and took inventory. Half a carton of one-percent, four eggs, one of them slightly cracked, bagged salad that was several days past sell-by, Sasha's diet cream, three limp carrots and a few strips of bacon.

Instead of working on various ways of positioning her bookshelves, she started another grocery list, this time with a man in mind. She might be able to live on salad, peanut butter and ice cream, but if Cole was going to be moving in…

Good gravy, Cole was moving in? Into her *house?*

Out of the question. She'd sooner take her chances with a stalker, who probably wasn't one, anyway. Probably a telemarketer who forgot to pay his phone bill and was forced to make his calls in person. Or a spammer whose computer crashed.

One thing she could almost guarantee—if she let Cole Stevens move in with her, she was going to want him in her bed, and that was about as dumb as facing down a deadline by ripping her house apart.

She wrote down *pork chops, potatoes,* and then began doodling while her mind drifted off down fantasy lane. She wasn't the only one who had enjoyed that kiss. Some things a man couldn't hide, enthusiastic arousal being one of them.

Maybe she'd better plow through her boxes and dig out all the erotica titles. After reading the first few she hadn't bothered to read any more. Her tastes ran to more plot and less sex.

G-spots? That mythical so-called "little death" that was supposed to potentially render a woman unconscious for a few seconds?

Forget it. She liked fiction as well as the next person, but she preferred hers to be reality-based. If any man ever got close to her G-spot—that is, if she even had one—to heck with losing consciousness, she wanted to be awake to enjoy it while it lasted.

Meanwhile, she'd better quit fantasizing and get busy.

Some forty-five minutes later she opened the door to Cole and a rush of cold, damp air.

"No callers?" he asked, dropping a six-pack and two plastic sacks on the hall bench.

"Nope. And you know what? The more I think about it, the more certain I am that it's just someone who's new to the area, who's just trying to learn his way around town."

"Using you for a guide? Why not just pick up a map?"

"A map of what? Metropolitan Muddy Landing?"

"Yeah, I guess you're right. It's not exactly the Greater Norfolk area."

"Or even the Greater Elizabeth City area." To keep from staring at his mouth, his shoulders, his chest or anything south of the border—*Lord help me, I'm out of control!*—Marty frowned at his hair and said, "You got a haircut." It sounded more like an accusation than an observation.

"Homemade. Why, did I miss a spot?" When she didn't reply, he went on to say, "Look, I've got what it takes to install chains on both your doors and stops on all the first-floor windows so they can't be raised from the outside. It's far from perfect, but this guy doesn't strike me as an expert."

"Slow up—wait a minute! You're talking like we've got a real crime wave here. I'm sorry now I ever mentioned that damn gray Mercedes."

There must be some law of physics that dictated that the more she overreacted, the more he underreacted. Here she was, flapping her arms like a scarecrow in a windstorm, while he stood there, calm as a marble statue.

"Like I said," he put in quietly once she shut up and stopped flapping, "it's probably nothing, but as long as I bought all this stuff, you might as well put it to use. Once you open for business again, a few precautions make sense."

Calm down. Deep breath. "You mean in case some dumb creep tries to break in and loot my cash drawer? He'd be lucky to find lunch money."

"Insurance won't pay off unless you can prove you've taken certain precautions."

She crossed her arms while she tried to find some flaw in his line of reasoning. The truth was that she should have thought of it herself. She might be casual about her home because she knew her neighbors—her neighborhood—but a business was something else.

"How much did all that stuff cost?" she growled.

He reminded her that it was a legitimate business deduction and handed her the sales slips. "You don't like to lose an argument, do you." Again that twitchy little smile.

That was the trouble with enigmatic men—you could never be certain what went on behind their manly composure.

"Who does?" she countered, waiting for him to fire his next shot. It occurred to her that arguing with Cole Stevens was nowhere near as depressing as arguing with a husband. She and Alan had rarely argued, they'd simply drifted apart…that is, until his illness had brought them together again.

With Beau, it had been different. Beau always started out by wheedling, turning nasty only when he couldn't get his way. Besides his charming self, Beau had brought to the marriage a vintage Jag, a few really nice antiques and several beautiful and no doubt valuable gilt-framed paintings. All but the Jag were gone within the first year, sold to pay off his gambling debts. He'd claimed it wasn't his fault he was always in debt—he was an addict, and addicts couldn't be held responsible, and if she loved him, she wouldn't keep refusing to change the deed on the house. He'd held to that argument right up until she'd had the good sense to kick him out of her house and her life.

But when Cole argued he simply stated the facts and then waited for her to see reason. The crazy thing was that arguing with Cole was stimulating—almost like a sport.

She put the beer in the fridge, then followed him from door to door, window to window while he installed the new hardware, handing him tools and trying to ignore the quiet, efficient way he moved. The way the muscles in his forearms flexed as he twisted the screwdriver.

"Remember, none of this is any good if you don't use it," he warned.

"You don't have to state the obvious. I promise to latch the chains and flip the little brass whatchamacallit on all the windows before I go to bed every night."

Something else to add to her growing list of things to do. So far the list included making sure she turned off everything that needed turning off; making sure the commode wasn't running—it had a tendency to hang up; and slathering on the miracle cream she'd wasted money on because it promised her a dewy, well-moisturized, line-free complexion. How exciting could life get for a woman whose sole interest at the moment was rehabilitating a moribund career?

Marty got out the broom and dustpan while Cole put his tools on the step to go upstairs.

Hands on his hips, he said, "They're not foolproof, but at least you'll have enough of a heads-up to call nine-one-one and get the hell out of the house."

They headed back to the kitchen, which no longer reeked of polyurethane and blackened cinnamon. "Outdoors? But that's where our mythical stalker will be waiting," Marty protested. She would much rather wrap herself in those strong, tanned arms and ignore the whole crazy mess. "You know what? The trouble is, I read too much. Instead of suspense, from now on maybe I'll stick to—" She'd been about to say romances, but then, those weren't the safest reading, either. Not when there was a genuine cover-worthy hero standing only a few feet away. "Biographies," she finished weakly. "I'm pretty sure I just overreacted."

He didn't say a word. Didn't have to—his eyes said it for him.

The first time she'd seen him she'd thought he looked wild, windblown and untamed, like the swashbuckling hero on the cover of a historical romance. Now that she'd come to know him better, he looked…

That was the trouble. He *still* looked like a swashbuckler, only now she saw more than just broad shoulders, narrow hips, greenish eyes that saw far too much, and all that shaggy, sun-streaked hair. Now his appeal was all tied up in a hundred small details, like the soapy, salty scent of his tanned skin and his deep raspy drawl. Like the way he held doors for her and helped her in and out of his monster truck. The way his lips twitched and his eyes crinkled when he was amused, but reluctant to admit it. The way he kissed…

Oh, my mercy, the way he kissed. What on earth was going on inside her small-town, dull-as-mud, semi-educated brain? He should have known better than to start anything he wasn't willing to finish.

Because she *was* willing. Far too willing. The trouble was, the job came with a built-in deadline, and her carpenter came with the job, and any distractions could royally screw up her schedule.

Right. And don't you forget it.

She reminded herself that elevated stress levels were only to be expected under the circumstances. Genuine clinical depression was another thing altogether. She didn't have time to be depressed. She certainly couldn't afford a shrink, and talking it over with her best friends wasn't even a faint possibility. She knew in advance what that pair would recommend.

Bracing her shoulders, she said, "Okay—for insurance purposes, but I still think all this might be overkill."

"Maybe. But like I said, if you hear someone messing around outside, it'll give you time to call nine-one-one."

"Betty Mary Crotts—she's the night dispatcher—she's another of my regulars. If she happens to be awake, she'll probably have her nose in a Regency romance."

"All the more reason to keep you safe. Your regulars need you."

"There's just no winning an argument with you, is there." It sounded almost like a compliment. From the twinkle in his eyes, he knew it, too. Damn him for reading her like a third-grade primer. "Then shall we both get to work? We've already wasted half the day."

"Wasted?"

She couldn't meet his eyes. Instead, she snatched up her floor-plan-in-progress and stalked off toward the living room.

They ate lunch separately. Shortly after Cole went back to work, Marty called up the stairway to say she was going to run to the post office and would be back in an hour or so. She didn't wait to hear his arguments. If a certain Mercedes wanted to follow her while she picked up her mail, plus a few things she needed from the drugstore, all the better. She would damn well force a confrontation and end this silly charade once and for all.

She slowed down as she passed the Caseys' brick ranch. They'd driven his car to Florida. Hers was locked in the garage.

No sign of a Mercedes as she drove to the post office to collect her daily allotment of catalogs and bills. She traded greetings with Miss Canfield, whose tremors were getting worse. "Are you having a garden this year?" she asked.

"Just beans, tomatoes and okra."

"Let me know if you have any trouble with deer. I've found something that works pretty well."

At the drugstore she smiled and nodded to Mr. Horton who lived in the same trailer park as Faylene. Judging from the books he read, the old man was considerably more adventurous than he looked.

Marty headed for the middle aisle where she picked up a bottle of ibuprofen and a microwaveable heat pack in case her lower back started acting up again. Passing the cosmetics display, she impulsively picked out a frosted pink blusher.

And then she saw the condoms.

Oh, for heaven's sake.

All the same, what if…?

A few minutes later she walked out with the blusher, the back-wrap, a bottle of ibuprofen and a box of condoms. With her cheeks burning like fire, she hardly needed the blusher.

It was late afternoon by the time she got back home, having stopped by the bank to order checks for Marty's New and Used at the new address. If everything went according to schedule she would soon be needing them.

Bursting through the front door, she met Cole coming down the stairs with a stack of broken plasterboard. "I told you to toss that stuff out the bedroom window. You don't have to be so careful. I can clean up."

"No problem," he said coolly.

His brusque response did little to quench her optimism. "You know what? I'm going to meet my deadline."

He nodded and waited for her to open the door for him.

She did, and then stood there like a lamppost, clutching her catalogs and her drugstore purchases.

"In case you were worried," she said when he came back inside, "I'm keeping track of all the time you've spent on extras." When he greeted the news with only the lift of one dark eyebrow, she hurried to explain. "I mean stuff that wasn't in our contract."

"Trade it for a few meals. Just remember what I said."

What the devil was bugging him? Remember *what?* She was having trouble remembering her own name at the moment.

"Oh, you mean if I hear someone trying to break in, I'm to call Betty Mary. Got it."

"And then call me."

"Why? You'll be miles away, sound asleep in your boat, and anyway, the local law can handle it. In case they're late and someone does manage to break in, I'll lean over the banisters and drop books on his head." She tried out a perky smile just because he looked so grim.

"Dammit, Marty, I'm serious!"

"Well, you don't have to yell at me. I just meant I could stall him until help arrives. Of course, paperbacks might not do the job. Heavy literature might work better." She was deliberately being facetious and she didn't really know why. Because she was embarrassed? Because she was still clutching her packages, including the box of condoms? Because what she really wanted was for her swashbuckling carpenter to ride in on a white stallion, sweep her off her feet and save her from the bad guys?

That didn't even make sense. What evildoer worth the title drove around town at twelve miles an hour in an elderly Mercedes? The thing didn't even have tinted windows.

As if he had all the time in the world, Cole hooked his thumbs in the low waist of his jeans and waited for a reaction. All eight remaining fingers pointed toward ground zero. When Marty realized she was staring she quickly lifted her gaze in time to see his lips twitch, but when no smile was forthcoming, she thought maybe she'd just imagined it.

Why the heck wasn't the man easier to read? He was a carpenter, for Pete's sake, not one of those superheroes who managed to save the world with one hand tied behind him. The type who could last all weekend in bed without the benefit of any little blue pills.

"Well. That pretty well settles it, then, wouldn't you say?" she huffed. It was the best she could come up with. He could take it any darn way he wanted to.

Oh, yes, that was definitely amusement she saw sparkling in those eyes. If he laughed at her she'd kill him.

He didn't laugh. Soberly, he said, "There's only one more thing I need to do."

She was afraid to ask.

"You might as well come with me to the marina while I throw a few things in a bag. We can pick up some barbecue on the way back."

She took a step back and bumped into the hall bench. Once a klutz, always a klutz. "Oh, now wait a minute, maybe we'd better rethink this—what you said earlier. About spending the night here. Most of my second floor, in case you haven't noticed, is pretty well uninhabitable." Since she'd moved into the spare room, her old bedroom—the one that would soon be her new living room—was the repository for roughly a ton of paperback books, not to mention stacks of assorted building material.

"I'll sleep on the sofa."

She said, "Ha! I can just see you leaping up to go into action with a hammer and screwdriver against an armed intruder."

That drew both a twitch *and* a twinkle. "Just don't go dropping any books on my head if I need to use the john in the middle of the night."

All she could do was shake her head. Wasn't being broke and racing to beat a deadline so she could do something about it enough excitement, without throwing in car chases and sexy carpenters? Who the devil was plotting this life of hers, anyway?

"Another benefit," he said calmly, "is that I won't waste so much traveling time. I can get started as soon as we walk Mutt, and work as late as necessary, or at least until you go up to bed."

It made sense…sort of. "You really do think I need a bodyguard, then?"

"Let's just say it's better to be safe than sorry."

"To coin a cliché," she murmured. "All right, then, but if the perp tries to climb in a window and tramples on my iris bulbs, he's going to wish he'd tackled some other mark. Believe me, I'm not helpless."

This time his amusement was unmistakable. "Right. All those boxes of ammo upstairs. Three guesses which ones you've been reading."

Even if he was laughing at her, it felt good. A kind of warm-and-mushy-inside good. If she had an ounce of survival instinct, she'd be out of here retroactively, stalker or no stalker. Because the real enemy was inside her gates. A Trojan horse of another color.

Marty was used to arguing with her female friends. It

was the way they bounced ideas off each other when they were trying to come up with the best way to get a couple of needy people together. Nobody's feelings ever got hurt. With Alan, they'd been too much alike to argue, even before he got sick. More like best friends—or later, like mother and child.

Arguments with Beau had occasionally been about backgrounds; her lack of one and his illustrious one. More often they had been about money. Win or lose, she'd always ended up depressed. If anyone had told her it was possible to argue with a man and actually enjoy it, she'd have said they were nuts.

It was after dark when they set off. Cole had hammered and sawed and done his thing upstairs, while Marty had worked on her prospective layout downstairs. Sasha would insist on feng shui along with her three shades of red. Paint was one thing, but Marty didn't have room for any feng shui. Her biggest concern was having as many books as possible exposed to as many browsers as possible, all without threatening claustrophobia.

The night was cold and luminous, the three-quarter moon set in a bed of iridescent clouds. They came to a section of soybean fields where the sky was visible practically from horizon to horizon, and Cole slowed almost to a stop. There was no traffic.

"North Star. Check it out."

"Where?" Leaning forward against the seat belt to peer through the windshield, Marty tried to summon up her meager knowledge of astronomy. Thanks to a passing interest in astrology, she knew the names of the planets, but not how to find them.

"See the Big Dipper over by that dead tree?" He waited until she said she did. "Now draw an imaginary line through the two stars at the end of the bowl and there's your North Star."

"I see it, I see it! I'm impressed."

"Yeah," he said smugly. "That's what I'm shooting for. I figured once you found out how smart I was, you'd jump to do my bidding without any more backtalk."

In the faint light of the dashboard, she stared at his just-this-side-of-handsome profile. "Balderdash."

He picked up speed and cut her a quick glance. "Balderdash?"

"It's a literary term. It means bull-pucky."

"Pucky?" He was openly laughing at her now, teeth flashing white in his tanned face.

Crossing her arms over her chest, Marty said, "You know very well what I mean." But then she was laughing, too.

"Looks like Bob Ed's entertaining tonight," he observed a few minutes later as they turned off onto a dirt road that led past the guide's home-office.

"He's surprisingly gregarious for a grizzled old bachelor. I think Faylene might have something to do with it."

They drove slowly along the waterfront, past several short piers to the one on the end where a low-profile boat was secured to the wooden pilings.

"Welcome to the *Time Out*," Cole said, quiet pride evident in his tone.

The deck dipped precariously when she stepped aboard, clutching his hand for balance.

"Easy there, I've got you."

"It's hardly the first time I've ever been on a boat," she

said, trying not to grab him and hang on with both hands. "I rode the ferry to Ocracoke several summers ago, and I've even been deep-sea fishing."

That was the time when one of Sasha's clients invited the decorator and any of her friends who cared to join her to spend a day fishing in the Gulf Stream. She'd been too busy throwing up to appreciate the thousand-dollar treat.

"My, it's...airy, isn't it?" she murmured, holding tightly to a stanchion while Cole unlocked a door and led her belowdeck.

When he turned on lights, she looked around, marveling at the way everything seemed to fit together.

"For an older model, she's in great shape. I've been working on her in my spare time for years," Cole said as he opened and closed various lockers.

Marty continued to look around, curious about what it was that led a man like Cole Stevens to live aboard a boat. It could hardly be called a yacht, but his pride was obvious—even touching.

His hands came down on her shoulder and he shifted her aside in order to open the door to the tiny head. Marty was struck by the same clean, masculine scent she'd come to associate with him. She was no expert on male toiletries, but whatever brand he used, it was nothing at all like the products used by either of her husbands. Alan had favored Old Spice, claiming it reminded him of his father. Beau had doused himself in a potent cologne that she'd quickly come to despise.

"I haven't been down this way in months," Marty said once they left the *Time Out* and headed back to Muddy Landing. "Not since Bob Ed's last birthday bash, in fact."

Cole slowed outside the guide's living quarters, where

a flickering blue light shone through the windows. Watching basketball, probably. Faylene was an avid sports fan.

"That's Faylene's car. You met her, didn't you? She's promised to come once I'm ready to open and help with a final cleaning."

"Blond lady in a pink sequined sweatshirt and white tennis shoes? I met her."

The description was a lot kinder than some she'd heard. Summer or winter, Faylene's unique fashion sense tended to raise eyebrows in those who didn't know her.

Cole slowed as they neared the turnoff. Where the wooden wharf followed the shoreline, a few commercial fishing boats glowed dimly in the moonlight. At the very end, a sleek, dark-hulled yacht rode quietly on the still water. A couple of cars and trucks, rentals most likely, were parked between a stack of crab pots and a chain hoist. Some marina operators kept a few rentable wrecks on hand for layovers.

Cole said, "In case you wondered how I managed to bring both my boat and a truck south, this is one of Bob Ed's rentals. Things are slow, so I got the pick of the litter."

"That explains the rod holders on the front bumper, then," she murmured drowsily.

"Yep. I troll—I rarely surf fish."

This time she didn't bother to comment, lulled by the sound of the tires and the steady presence beside her.

"Barbecue?" he asked a few minutes later as he pulled onto Highway 168 again.

She opened her eyes and yawned. "Sounds good. Tomorrow I need to make a trip to the grocers."

"How about we run by after we do the dog in the morning."

She was too relaxed to bother arguing. At this rate, she thought sleepily, her remodeling job was going to take a back seat to all the other activities, and as much as she enjoyed them, she couldn't afford any more delays. "How about you carp while I walk Mutt and do the shopping?"

"We'll see," he said agreeably.

"Damn right we will," she muttered, but there was no fire in it. Only slumbering coals. If she didn't watch out, her priorities were going to be turned end for end, and the worst thing about it was that she found the threat more exciting than frightening.

Eight

How's a woman supposed to concentrate, Marty asked herself, when her sleeping dragon wakes up after a long winter's nap, only to trip over a sexy dragon-slayer?

Okay, bad analogy. She didn't think too clearly this early in the morning. Never had, actually, but now it was even worse. Now she was hungover after wrestling with a night full of X-rated dreams. Inviting Cole to move in with her had been a major mistake.

Although, come to think of it, she'd never actually issued an invitation.

Wet-haired and bleary-eyed, she made her way downstairs at a quarter of seven on Friday morning and shoved open the kitchen door. And there he was, seated at her table—the star of all those steamy high-definition dreams.

Slowly, he unfolded his taut, muscular body as she entered his room, his narrowed eyes taking in every detail, from her towel-dried hair to her grubby cross-trainers. Four of his square-tipped fingers rested on the tabletop. "You look pale. Sure you're feeling all right? Was it the barbecue?"

Heck no, she wasn't feeling all right. Barbecue had nothing to do with it. She hadn't felt this "not all right" since she'd flunked algebra on account of the boy who sat in front of her, whose voice had already changed and who had had to shave at least twice a week.

She tried to think of something marginally intelligent to say and came up empty. "Sorry 'f I woke you. Tried to be quiet," she mumbled. Her early morning voice was raspy to the point of surliness, but then he already knew that. Any friend who knew her well enough to drop in before noon understood. "Not a morning person. It's January—February—whatever. I'm still hibernating."

Cole nodded. Didn't say a word but looked as if he understood. Sympathy, she didn't need. Sympathy always made her combative. When he continued to stand, she waved him back to his seat. "Just don't expect me to carry on a conversation," she warned.

Silent as an oyster, he nodded again.

She was the only one who was doing any conversing, and for some reason she couldn't seem to shut up. "Circadian rhythms," she grumbled as if that explained everything. Opening a cabinet, she stared at a box of dry cereal, made a face and shut the door. One thing about walking Super-Mutt—it not only woke up her appetite, it helped oxygenate her brain.

Cole sat down again and tipped his chair back. Not saying a word. Just sitting there, watching while she muttered about circadian rhythms.

"It's just that as soon as I get things sorted out," she felt compelled to explain, "we go on daylight saving time and the whole stupid process starts all over again. If I had half a brain I'd find myself a night job. Maybe a convenience store…"

Chatter, chatter, chatter. So much for not being a morning person. She was okay with Sasha and Faylene, who knew her limitations and made allowances, but with anyone else she was hopeless.

She fumbled in the dish cabinet for her favorite mug, wishing she had her house to herself again.

Liar, liar, pants on fire!

Nobody should look that good this early. The brass lamp over the table shone down on his head, making his hair glisten with moisture. He must have already showered. Which meant he'd been standing there stark naked only a few feet away from where she was sleeping. No wonder she'd woken up panting and throbbing.

"What ever happened to the sun?" she muttered.

"It's on the way. Give it a few more minutes." He reached for the drawing pad that was spread open alongside his coffee mug, while Marty filled her mug from the fresh pot of coffee, the fumes of which were just now reaching her caffeine receptors. She added two heaping sugars and a dollop of milk.

"Toast, or something more substantial?" he asked genially as if she hadn't practically snarled at him.

She focused on the two slices of whole-wheat waiting at half-mast in the toaster. "No solids, not this early."

Clearing her throat, she asked him what he was working on, and Cole slid the pad over so she could see it. She stared at the lines on the paper until the elegant drawing began to make sense. "Nice," she murmured. "Compact. Not exactly what you'd call a family room, but I guess it's all there."

Which was actually a fairly coherent response, all things considered.

Okay, so he could draw as well as take things apart and put them back together again. He could talk about things like coffee and toast and still manage to look like the kind of guy who devoured fair maidens for breakfast.

She took another rejuvenating sip of coffee, sat her mug on the table and cleared her throat. "Cole…am I making a monumental mistake here?"

His eyes widened. The dark centers seemed to expand.

"What we're doing upstairs, I mean."

She closed her eyes, Not *that,* she nearly said, stopping herself just in time. They hadn't done a darn thing upstairs—not together, at least. If you didn't count a few territorial skirmishes.

Leaning back, he thumbed his freshly shaved chin and studied the drawing. He'd even gone so far as to indicate a small ceiling fixture over the table. "What's the matter—you're having second thoughts?"

"Only a million or so," she confessed.

"A little late, isn't it?"

"Actually, it's too early. I usually sleep until seven-thirty or so, but since I've been walking the dog, I have to get up in the wee hours."

"Any reason why he can't wait until later in the day?"

Deep breath. Oxygenate that old brain. "Annie said he liked to go out for his first run before breakfast, but that might be so they could both get to work on time." Two slices of medium-crisp whole-wheat toast popped up, and without thinking she reached for the butter and the fig preserves. A little sugar rush wouldn't hurt, since she was being forced to sound rational before she was even awake.

With Sasha, who often dropped by on her way to work, depending on where her current client was located, Marty could be as grumpy as she liked. Her friend understood and never took it personally.

With Cole it was different. She hated for him to see her as she really was—a puffy-eyed, raspy-voiced going-on-thirty-seven-year-old woman.

Oh, yeah? How do you want him to see you? Naked and in his bed, all ready for a few rounds of whoopee?

Shut up, dammit, who asked you?

Who just bought a whole box of condoms?

Still tipped back, with his long legs stretched out before him, he said, "I haven't started on the cabinets yet. If you're not comfortable with the plans we agreed on, now's the time to say so. I can put things back the way they were, but it'll take a few days."

"I'm not," she protested quickly. "That is, I am. Comfortable, that is."

What she was not comfortable with was sharing breakfast with him, smelling his aftershave, his soap—actually her soap. He'd evidently forgotten to bring his own.

That was the trouble with dreaming the kind of dreams she didn't even know how to dream—it left her imagination susceptible to the slightest provocation. One whiff of the same brand of bath soap she'd used for years and she instantly pictured a naked carpenter standing in her shower with water streaming down on his broad shoulders, his narrow hips, his taut butt, his—

Okay, got the picture.

"No, it looks great," she croaked earnestly. "Really. I like what you've done here—this little space over the sink."

"In most kitchens you'd have a window there. You don't want a cabinet in your face."

She didn't particularly want a mirror in her face, either. "There's no room for a dishwasher, I guess." She had one, but never used it. Living alone, she ran out of clean dishes before she could ever get a full load. "That's okay. I'd probably never use it anyway."

"It might come in handy for holiday entertaining."

"Just make room for a double sink, that's all I need."

For no reason at all, he smiled at her across the table then, and she got tangled up in his eyes. His laugh lines, even his squint lines were sexy. Pity the same couldn't be said for her own. Double standards were the pits.

"Finish your toast and let's pick up Mutt. You think he's truck trained?"

"You mean, like housebroken?"

"I mean, if we anchor him in the back of my truck, will he try to jump out?" Rising, Cole reached for the coffee-pot, shot her a questioning look and, when she shook her head, switched it off. He glanced at the back door, and see-ing the chain still in place, set his mug in the sink and put away the butter, cream and preserves.

How the devil, Marty asked herself, could a man look sexy doing kitchen chores?

"In case your stalker shows up again, we might want to turn the tables and follow him. It'd be easier with wheels."

"Don't even think about it. All these chains and what-chamadoodles on the windows are one thing, but I didn't hire you as an extra in my tiny little melodrama."

"Not even as a walk-on? Not even if I agree to let Mutt have all the best lines?"

She couldn't help but laugh. What else could a woman do? Any way you looked at it, the man was irresistible.

"There, that's better," he said, pausing behind her chair to lay hands on the area where stress had her tight as a bowstring.

One of the areas, at least.

When his thumb began to work on her taut trapeziums she tipped her head back and closed her eyes.

In a soft voice that bordered on a growl he said, "We'd better get a move on. I like to be on the job by eight."

"I told you, there's no need for you to go with me. I've been walking him for a week. Now that I know how to control him, I don't need you."

As if she hadn't spoken, he said, "You want to run upstairs before we leave?"

"We. It's always first person singular when it comes to what you're doing upstairs, but the royal 'We' when it comes to everything else."

He nodded judiciously. "Sounds about right," he said just solemnly enough so that she knew he was joking.

"You're a chauvinist, you know that, don't you?" Brushing his hands away, she got up, rinsed her mug and plopped it in the drainer.

Hips braced against a counter, he grinned. "What tipped you off?"

She felt like frapping him with the hand towel. Instead, she dried her hands and reached for the bottle of jasmine-scented lotion on the shelf behind the sink. Then he got out both their coats and held hers while she slid her arms through the sleeves. She could feel him grinning at her as if she had eyes in the back of her head.

By the time they got out to the truck, the eastern sky was streaked with gold. *February,* she thought. *That's almost spring. Pretty soon it will be summer, and by then I'll be back in business.*

And where would Cole be, cruising down the intrastate waterway? Tied up at another marina, tearing up and rebuilding some other woman's house? For some reason spring didn't feel quite so promising.

The walk went surprisingly well, even after Marty insisted on taking charge of Mutt. The only time things threatened to get out of control was when a pack of strays showed up and the dog went crazy, yapping and jumping, ignoring her shouts, which of course he couldn't hear.

"I forgot how to make him look for my signals," she exclaimed when Cole stood back, making no move to take control.

"Give the leash a sharp jerk," he said.

She did. When Mutt looked around as if to say, "Wha-at?" Marty sliced off a hand signal, the rough translation of which was *Straighten up and fly right or I'll pull your eyelashes out!*

"That dog must be in heat," Cole said when they resumed the brisk pace.

Not that she'd give him the satisfaction of saying it, but Marty hated to think what would have happened if she'd been alone. "Yeah, I figured that's all it was."

"Probably going to be some free pups in a few months. You did say you're thinking of getting a dog?"

"No time soon," she said grimly, shortening the leash when Mutt got a little too interested in inspecting the tires on a rusty Fairlane that was parked illegally. "Speaking of time, we can head back now. It'll be a full half hour by the time we get to the kennel."

"Honor system?"

"Darn right," she said. "Besides, he's a big guy. He needs the exercise."

Outside the canine boarding house, Cole reached for the leash. "You want to wait in the truck while I take him inside?"

"No, thanks." She was cool. In control. Mutt was seated on his overgrown haunches, grinning up at her as if to say *You go, girl!*

So what did Cole Stevens do?

The one thing designed to shatter her composure. Laying a hand on her, he leaned over and kissed her.

Right there in broad daylight, in front of a stream of traffic. Or if not exactly a stream, at least a bread delivery van, a bicycle and Susie-at-the-bank's new hatchback.

Oh, my, if she'd been turned on by his looks, by his voice and his touch, his taste sent her sailing over the edge. Whose heart was it that was thundering between them? Beating hard enough to be felt even through two layers of coat? His or hers?

Or both?

They were standing toe to toe. One of his hands moved up to her back, holding her close. The familiar taste of him—coffee, mint and something essentially personal, was as intoxicating as any whiskey.

Not until he stepped away did Marty realize that she had a death grip on his arms. She stepped back, forced herself to breathe normally and tried pinning on a smile. Her lips were tingling. She only hoped they weren't trembling.

Cole licked his lips and said casually, "Mmm, nice. Coconut?"

But his eyes had gone dark on her again. She took a modicum of satisfaction in that, at least.

A red convertible was parked behind her minivan when they got back to Sugar Lane, so Cole parked on the street. "Pretty early for company," he observed.

"Not for Sasha," Marty replied, not sounding particularly happy at the prospect of company. "She stops by on her way to work sometimes."

There were two women seated in the car. As the top was up, Cole couldn't tell much about them. Leaving Marty to invite them inside—or not—he headed toward the front door. As the door was locked and the key was in her coat pocket instead of under the doormat—he'd insisted on that—he had no choice but to wait.

A minute later both car doors opened and two women emerged. He'd met the redhead before, but not the tall blonde in black pants, black boots, a long, black coat and a purple chenille scarf.

The three women trooped up the front walk, the blonde carefully stepping on each flagstone, the redhead striding out in front, ignoring stepping stones and whatever it was that was shooting up beside the walk. Looked like onions. Probably wasn't.

"Hi, Cole. Lily, this is Marty's carpenter." Short yellow fur coat, black tights and all, the height-challenged redhead charged up the steps, right hand extended. There was at least one ring per finger, including her thumb. "I'm Sasha, remember? We met the other day?"

As if anyone was likely to forget.

By that time Marty and the blonde had made it to the front door. Sasha said, "Lily and I were on our way to

IHOP, and it occurred to me that since Marty's going to be opening again right here in the neighborhood, she might need some professional advice. Home office and all—the IRS is picky about that sort of thing. Believe me, I work out of my home, so I know all about it. They make you jump through flaming hoops, right, Lily?"

"I'm sure Ms. Owens is familiar with the regulations." Her voice, Cole decided, matched her looks. Cool, competent, with an air of superiority that might or might not be merited.

The talk of business records and home offices continued briefly before turning to more general topics. Then the redhead hit him with a few personal questions, to which he gave only minimal answers.

Did he actually live aboard a boat?

Yeah, he did. No, it definitely wasn't a yacht, and yes, he'd met Faylene Beasley. No, he didn't have children, and yes, if he had, he would definitely teach them to swim before they could walk.

Yada-yada-yada. Funny thing, though—even as he was answering her nosy questions, he couldn't help but notice that she seemed more interested in Marty's reaction than to anything he was saying.

The blonde looked cool, even in a long black topcoat that Cole recognized as being a pricey model. Among other things, Paula had taught him something about women's clothing. Without making an issue of it, Ms. Sullivan glanced at a tank watch that Cole recognized as a Tiffany model, either that or a damned good knock-off.

Sasha tapped him on the shoulder. "I suppose you know a lot of people around here, hm? Is that why you decided to lay over here? That is what you call it, isn't it? Laying over?"

"Yes, ma'am, I believe that's what it's called."

"Oh, would you just listen to that! Honey, you're so un-PC you're adorable!"

Cole had taken about all he could take without triggering his gag reflex. Before he could think of a reply that would deflect her attention without being openly rude, she turned away.

"Marty, in case you have any questions, you know who to call. Now remember what I told you about colors. You're not going to have that much wall exposed, so you've got to make every inch work for you." Before Marty could respond, Sasha turned back to Cole. "It's great seeing you again. Faylene's told me so much about you and those lovely windows you put in for Bob Ed."

Lovely windows? Unpainted secondhand double-hung windows in an unpainted building? What the devil had the Beasley woman said about him, anyway? He'd spoken to her for three minutes, tops.

Marty opened the door and more or less hurried them out, promising they'd get together for lunch one day soon. Cole was still trying to figure out what had just happened—hell, it was barely eight in the morning—when he heard the plump little redhead who was striding off down the front lawn saying, "That went well, doncha think? Did you see the way she—"

He didn't catch the rest because Marty slammed the door shut. Oh, boy, the lady was steamed about something. Probably wouldn't do much good to ask, but he asked anyway. "Did I miss something important?"

"What? Oh—no. Yes. I mean, I don't know if you realize it or not, but you're now an official target."

"Whoa, I'm not sure I like the sound of that." He backed a few steps toward the stairway.

"Depends on whether or not you like gorgeous, intelligent, independent women," she snapped. "That's who they're setting you up with."

"Now wait a minute—who's setting me up? How?"

"With Lily. Why else would Sasha bring her by here this early when she knows I'm not even coherent this time of day?" Her cheeks were burning, her soft gray eyes flashing fire. "It's not me and my tax situation they're interested in. No way—it's you."

"Hey, I hardly spoke three words to the woman," Cole protested. "By now she's probably already forgotten my name."

"Don't kid yourself," Marty said dryly.

What the devil was she so steamed about? If she already had an accountant, all she had to do was say so. If anyone had a reason to be steamed, it was he. For a few minutes there he'd felt like he had a target painted on his chest.

"Let's get to work, all right? We've wasted enough time."

Nine

In a cheerfully cluttered room a few hours later, Sasha eased off her five-inch heels and massaged her size-five feet. "Now I know how a ballerina must feel. Oh, quit fussing around! Sit down and talk to me," she exclaimed. "No point in washing the inside when the outside's spattered with winter grunge."

Dutifully, Faylene set aside her spray bottle of window cleaner and the wad of crumpled newspapers. "Next warm spell we have I'll get 'em all done, inside and out. I got me one of them things you screw on to a hose. You ready for iced tea?"

"In the fridge. Pour us both a glass, will you?" Sasha eased her feet up onto the sofa. For the few minutes the housekeeper was out of the room, she let herself sag against the cushions. "Bring those macaroons, too," she called. Faylene had stopped by the bakery on her way to work. She was a whiz at cleaning, but her culinary skills were notorious, as everyone who'd ever employed her quickly discovered.

With refreshments on hand, the two women got down to brass tacks. Faylene touched her Dolly Parton do to make sure the lacquered surface was still intact. "What'd she think?"

"Lily? Who knows? Maybe you can find out, I couldn't get a thing out of her."

"Comes from filling out all them gov'ment forms all day long. She don't talk to me, neither, and I been cleanin' for her goin' on a year now."

"So far all I've been able to find out is that she graduated from Wharton, her father's in the military—probably pretty high rank, although I'm just guessing about that. Oh, and she hates country music."

"Bob Ed says Mr. Stevens's got a guitar on board that boat o' his." She pronounced it git-tawr.

"So we'll broaden her education." Sasha sipped her syrupy tea. "Today's country music was yesterday's folk music. If we tell her something like that, she might be more inclined to expand her horizons. But first he needs some incentive to hang around. That's where we come in."

"It still don't sound much like a match to me, her being college educated and all. Maybe we ought to look around some more. How 'bout one o' them highfalutin business men you work for."

"Married, gay or dull as mud. Don't underestimate our studly carpenter. A friend of mine knows the decorator who did his house, and she says—"

"What house? If he's got a house, why's he sleepin' aboard that old boat? It's not like it was a yacht or anything."

"According to my source, he used to be pretty high up

the ladder with this big development firm up in Virginia. In fact, he was married to his boss's daughter, but then there was some kind of scandal—business, not personal. Anyway, by the time the dust settled, he was out of a job, the company was down the drain and his wife and her lawyers cleaned him out. That's why he's living on board his boat and taking small jobs to make ends meet."

"I don't know 'bout meetin' no ends, but he didn't charge Bob Ed nothin' to fix his windows. Shelled out two weeks in advance for the wet slip, too."

"Even better. I doubt if Mar—that is, if Lily would be interested if he were truly down on his luck."

The light dawned. "Law heppus, it's Marty you're fixin' to match him up with, not Miss Lily." Faylene smirked, rearranging a face that had more wrinkles than a box of prunes.

"Well, what do you think? She hasn't had a man in years, not even a loaner."

"She's sure been awful crotchety lately."

"Mmm-hmm. And Lord knows, he's temptation on the hoof. By the way, are y'all planning your usual birthday bash this year?"

"Stewed goose with rutabagas, collards, barbecue and all the rest, same as always."

"All the rest meaning a supply of aged-in-the-jar moonshine," Sasha teased. It was the hunting guide's standard birthday bash, a tradition in an area where entertainment was usually of the homemade variety. It was also a golden opportunity for matchmaking. Sasha wouldn't miss it for anything. Last year's guest list had included a bank president, the chief of surgery at Chesapeake General and three

Tides players who were slated for big things in the majors, all clients of Bob Ed's—plus Faylene's special friends.

"Just don't wear them spike-heel shoes this time," the bouffant blonde warned. "You get one o' them things caught 'tween the planks on the dock and sic a lawyer on 'im, and Bob Ed's not gonna invite you to no more parties."

"I'll be sure to dress suitably for the occasion. Maybe I'll borrow a pair of your sneakers. But back to Cole Stevens—my source in Virginia said the wife was a real witch, so our hunky carpenter might be just a tad gun-shy."

"Name me a man that's not, 'specially if they think they're being herded into a corral."

"What about you and Bob Ed?"

"You don't see us rushin' to tie any knots, do you? And what about you? You had four husbands and not a one of 'em stuck around no longer'n it took for the ink to dry on the papers." The two women knew each other well enough to get down and dirty without giving or taking offense.

"How do you think I got to be such an expert? And anyway, we're hardly herding them to the altar—all we're doing is encouraging two nice people to take a second look at each other by putting them together in a different context," Sasha reasoned.

Faylene pursed her lips. Actually, they were more or less permanently pursed, as she drew the line at Botox injections. "There's some other fellers invited to the party. Maybe I'll invite Miss Lily and we can see what happens."

"Kill two birds with one stone, so to speak."

"Kill more'n that, if we get lucky. Bob Ed's invited them fellers from that fifty-five footer that tied up the other day." A born-and-bred local, Faylene referred to anything larger than a commercial fishing boat by its length rather than its name. "'You make sure Miss Lily comes, and I'll take care o' Marty."

"It's a deal," Sasha agreed, her expression that of a cream-fed Persian cat.

Marty considered asking Cole for help, but then she heard the whine of the power saw, reminding her that she needed him upstairs more than she did downstairs. She'd moved the damn things into the garage using only her back, her brain and a two-wheel hand truck. If she could just get this one past the single step and into the kitchen, the rest of the way would be easy.

After spending the winter outside, her poor minivan was going to appreciate having the garage to itself again, she thought as she levered the cut-down section of bookshelf onto the cart, balanced it and cautiously began moving backward toward the single step.

Ver-r-ry carefully, she backed up the step and tried to pull the cart up with her. When the damn thing started sliding, she let out a yelp.

Sudden silence from upstairs as the power saw cut off. Marty yelled again. Bracing her back on the door frame, she jammed one knee against the side of the shelf, hoping to keep it from toppling onto the cement garage floor. "Cole! Help me!"

"What in God's name—?" Like a genie out of a bottle, he appeared behind her. "Hang on, I'm coming!"

"You can't get past," she wailed, struggling in the doorway between kitchen and garage to steady the teetering bookcase.

He disappeared briefly. A few seconds later he reappeared in the garage, where he braced the leaning book-shelf with both hands. "What the devil were you trying to do? No, don't say anything. Steady now, I've got the shelf. When I tip it back, pull the cart up onto the kitchen floor, then wait until I come back around to take control."

The look she gave him was the rough equivalent of *Over my dead body.*

The cart was capable of moving a refrigerator as long as it was balanced. But a six-by-six-foot by eighteen-inch bookshelf was, by its very nature, unbalanced.

"Where the hell are you going with it, anyway?"

"Living room."

"Now? Why?"

She just shook her head. If she couldn't explain it to herself, she knew better than to try explaining it to anyone else. "Through here. Hold it while I take up the rug."

A few minutes later the first of the bookshelves was sharing space in the living room with a sofa, three chairs and two tables. It was monstrous.

It's a first step, she told herself. Every journey begins with a single step—she'd read that somewhere.

The trouble was, she'd read everything somewhere, at one time or another. Including Othello. One look at Cole, standing in the doorway, arms crossed over his chest, brought to mind another quotation. "Yon Cassio has a hungry look. Such men are dangerous."

And don't you forget it, she warned herself.

Struggling between discouragement and elation, she stared at the elephant in the drawing room. The rest of the herd was still in the garage. "I forgot how big it was," she whispered. "What am I going to do with all the others?"

"You're actually asking for suggestions? Wait until I have time to cut them down, and we'll make room in here."

Cole moved in behind her and put a hand on her shoulder. His thumb began smoothing away the tension that always seemed to gather at the back of her neck.

"Only trouble here is, you got the cart before the horse. Next time, ask for help."

"What I've got is a twenty-mule team before a buckboard. What you've got is work to do upstairs. I can manage down here."

She could manage a whole lot better if she weren't melting under his magic fingers. A puffy little sigh escaped her as he found the magic spot and began to work on it. Pain…but a good kind of pain…

"Don't be so damn stubborn," he chided.

"I'm not stubborn, but I know what has to be done and I don't see any reason to wait till the last minute to do it."

His hands left her shoulder and his arms slipped around her from behind.

"You're not stubborn. Rain's not wet. The temperature outside's not hovering around the freezing mark, either. Hey, it's almost spring out there, right? Flowers bursting out all over the place."

"All right, so I made a mistake. I should have moved all this stuff upstairs first, but I just wanted to get an idea of how it was going to look."

When he started to chuckle, she stiffened. "Don't say it. So now I've got a huge mess. I've probably made the biggest mistake of my life. Well, maybe the second biggest mistake."

His fingers were moving up the back of her neck to her

hair, stroking, massaging, sapping the strength from her aching bones.

He said, "What was the biggest? Just curious—you don't have to answer that."

"I don't intend to." He didn't need to know that she'd been on a romance-reading binge about the time she'd met Beau Owens. She'd mistaken suave manners, tailor-made suits and a Hollywood-handsome face for the real thing.

The only thing real about Beau had been his total lack of integrity. Wasn't there another quotation about a lesson too late for the learning?

Or no—that was a song, wasn't it?

She sniffed, wishing she had a tissue. Things were piling up too fast, flattening her hopes like a wet tortilla. Just yesterday she'd been happily working on floor plans. Sales counter here by the front window; old romances, billed as classics, in the dining room; new titles, once she could afford to stock them again, facing the entrance. A few posters, her autographed author pictures and maybe even those three-shades-of-red walls Sasha insisted would send customers into a buying frenzy.

Frenzy, my foot, she thought. So far all she'd accomplished was to destroy her single asset—her house. Her eyes blurred and then began to sting.

Without saying a word, Cole turned her so that she was leaning against him, damp-eyed and discouraged. And that was another thing—her emotions were all over the place. Either she wasn't eating right or sleeping enough, or she was sliding into early menopause. Now there was a cheerful thought!

"Hey," he murmured, his warm breath stirring her hair, "we got it this far, didn't we? What if I help you move your furniture upstairs right now? We'll leave your rocking chair here so you can sit and plan how you're going to use your space."

"We can't move upstairs yet—you're not finished up there." She almost wished he would quit being so helpful—so understanding. She was falling into the habit of depending on him, and that, she knew from experience, was a fatal mistake.

"We can throw sheets over the stuff to keep the dust off while I'm working. Until I finish your new kitchen you can still use the one down here, right?"

His tone was sympathetic, and unfortunately, sympathy had always been her undoing. She couldn't remember the last time she'd been undone, because her friends knew better than to push any of her emotional buttons. Once she started crying, which she absolutely refused to do, it was "man the lifeboats!"

He let her bawl her eyes out for several minutes, not even attempting to talk her out of it. Not once did he try to reason with her—not that it would have done a speck of good. His hands moved slowly over her back from shoulders to waist—no higher, no lower.

She sniffed. *Why on earth am I crying? I never cry!*

Her fingers crept across his chest, feeling to see if he had a tissue in his shirt pocket. He stiffened, and she suddenly became aware of the heat engendered by two warm bodies in close proximity. Of masculine hardness pressing against feminine softness. The scent of his skin only made matters worse. Instinctively, she moved against the hard ridge. Pelvis to pelvis. The hard ridge moved.

Omigracious!

She wasn't responsible for *that!* Couldn't be. She had it on the best of authority that she wasn't the type to turn men on. It was probably just a standard male reaction to the circumstances. Like—like—drinking beer and belching.

"There's a handkerchief in my hip pocket," he said, his voice sounding strained.

He was probably embarrassed and didn't know how to let go without hurting her feelings. So she did it for him. Stepped back and accepted the handkerchief he handed her.

And immediately missed his warmth, his strength, and everything else she'd been starved for, but hadn't realized it. She wiped, blotted and blew.

"I'll wash it," she said stiffly, avoiding his gaze.

He didn't say a word, just continued to look at her.

This is a dead-end road, woman. Stop right where you are.

And then he did just what she wanted most and needed least. He reached out and pulled her against him and… kissed her again.

This time there was no mistaking the nature of the kiss. It was carnal from the start. Without lifting his mouth from hers, he eased her past the bookshelf, backed her toward the sofa and lowered her onto the cushions.

It was hard and narrow with scarcely enough room for two to lie down unless they were plastered together. At first neither of them moved. The sensation that swept through her was one she hadn't felt in years. The mindless kind of hunger that demands immediate satisfaction.

Why couldn't she have bought a damn futon instead of a three-cushion couch? His backside had to be hanging off the edge. To keep him from landing on the floor, she anchored him by hooking a leg over his hip.

Smart move, Marty. Real subtle.

His hand grazed her breast as he eased the neck of her pullover away to nuzzle her collarbone. A rash of goose bumps broke out along her sides. How could he have known about that tiny hollow at the base of her throat? All he had to do was breathe on it and she fell apart.

His hands slipped under her sweater, under her bra. When his fingertips raked over her nipples, she whimpered, "We need to—to talk."

Will the last gray cell to leave the brain please turn out the lights?

Cole's hands went still. Talk? Was she crazy? More to the point, was he? If he was smart he'd get the hell out of here, contract or no contract, while he was still more or less in his right mind. He might drop anchor down around Southport, or maybe Charleston. Or maybe he'd just keep on the move until he couldn't remember her name or what she looked like, much less the way she smelled...or tasted.

He hadn't even begun to suspect how dangerous she was until the second day. Couldn't even remember what tipped him off. It wasn't as if she made any effort to attract him. No makeup, no heavy perfumes, just that flowery smelling soap and lotion.

"Marty," he said through clenched jaws, "I don't want to take advantage of you."

The hell he didn't! Crammed together on the hard-as-rocks cushions, with one thigh over his hips and her sweet little mound rubbing against his erection, he was about to explode.

What with work, worry, plus a hard narrow bunk in a cold cabin that smelled of mildew, Cole couldn't remember the last time he'd been in this condition. His libido had taken a sabbatical about the time he'd realized that Paula was cheating on him. Since then he'd been too busy to worry about getting laid.

The trouble was, this wasn't just a matter of getting laid. This was Marty.

So? She was a woman, wasn't she?

Unless he'd mistaken the signs, she was as eager as he was. And he just happened to have a condom in his wallet.

Right. One that had been there since around the time of his divorce, when he'd had some crazy notion of going out and snagging himself some revenge sex. The use-by date had probably long since expired.

She shifted and somehow managed to bring them into even closer contact where it counted. The crazy thing was that it counted everywhere. If he'd needed a reminder of just why sex with Marty Owens wasn't going to work, that was it. Not only because he worked for her, but because he liked her too much. Respected her. Hell, he even admired her. She was a little too independent for her own good, but then, there was probably a reason behind it.

"Marty—" He tried to ease away, but there was nowhere to go but the floor. He managed to slide off the sofa onto one knee, and felt stupid as hell. *Smooth, man. Really suave.*

"If you're looking for an apology," he said, the words grinding like a rusty hinge, "you've got it. I should never have—"

Sitting up, she laid a finger over his mouth. "Don't say it. Just don't, all right?" Her voiced sounded raw and her eyes refused to meet his.

He looked for other signs of vulnerability, but found none. Unless you counted the neck of her yellow sweater that was stretched out of shape, and the fact that her hair looked like she'd been through a wind tunnel.

With her chilly gray eyes focused somewhere over his left shoulder, she said primly, "Thank you very much for helping me get it in here."

A few wildly inappropriate notions zinged through his head before his brain reconnected. "Yeah, well…next time give me some warning. The short one shouldn't be a problem, though."

As he stood up he watched her face, trying to get a read on what was going on in that squirrelly mind of hers. It was like watching cloud shadows racing over the water, disguising what lay just under the surface.

"Yell when you want help moving this stuff upstairs," he said.

"Let me think about it first. Maybe this afternoon."

You'd think they were two strangers who just happened to be passing the time of day.

Shrugging, Cole climbed the stairs to finish what he'd been doing when he'd first heard her yell for help.

What *had* he been doing? His concentration was now shot, that was for damn sure. It didn't help that the bed she'd slept in last night was only a few feet away. His senses honed to a fine edge, he caught a whiff of the scented soap she used in the morning while she stood naked under the shower.

His power sander was waiting where he'd left it, a clue that he'd been working on her cabinet doors. He picked it up, reminding himself that power tools could be dangerous when a guy's blood deserted his brain and headed south.

Ten

Downstairs, Marty stared at the monstrous intrusion between her coffee table and the ugly platform rocker that was the first piece of furniture she'd ever bought.

My God, she'd almost—

And she'd wanted to. For the first time in more years than she cared to remember, she'd been ready to tear off her clothes and make love. Burning for it. Throbbing for it. She *never* burned, much less throbbed. And besides, her box of condoms was upstairs.

Deep breath. Another one. Now, back to the real world. It took some doing, but she did it, a measure of just how disciplined she could be when she put her mind to it.

After first removing the drawers, she maneuvered her desk through the living room, around the bookshelf, across the hall and into the kitchen, where it blocked the refrigerator. Shaking her aching hands, she told herself she'd find

a place for it later. It was only furniture, after all. She'd
learned early in life to keep her possessions to a minimum
and her goals realistic. Rearranging furniture was realistic. People did it all the time. If you didn't like the results,
you could always put things back the way they were.

The way they were? With a garage full of big empty
bookshelves, another one blocking her living room, not to
mention a ton of paperback books that were growing more
out-of-date by the minute?

And do not, she warned herself—I repeat, do *not* even
think about the man upstairs!

The maple drop-leaf dining table wasn't all that heavy
once she'd unloaded the to-be-read pile of books and the
to-be-dealt-with stack of mail, which was mostly catalogs,
anyway. By stacking the chairs, she managed to get all four,
plus the table, in the utility room. She'd have to clear them
all out to get to the washer, but it was the best she could
do for now. With more rain—possibly even sleet—in the
forecast, she could hardly set them out on the porch.

Hands on her hips, she surveyed the chaos. Was she
there yet? At the point of no return? Once she got past that
point, there'd be no going back. Until then she could still
fire her carpenter, put a hot plate in the bathroom, wash
dishes in the lavatory and use the refrigerator downstairs.

That was the trouble with having a galloping case of the
hots. It blew any possibility of logical thought.

Dammit, he wasn't even interested enough to take what
she'd offered. What did he want—time and a half for
overtime?

"Story of my life," she muttered, glaring at the dishes in
the sink that she had yet to wash and now couldn't get to
without climbing over a mountain of misplaced furniture.

Upstairs, the sound of a power sander continued, blocking out—she hoped—the sound of dragging and thumping, plus several four-letter words awkwardly strung together. Cursing was another area where she lacked expertise.

As she wandered back through her empty front rooms, Marty was surprised he hadn't come downstairs to see what was going on. "Aren't you even curious?" she muttered, eyeing her dusty staircase. "What are you afraid of? That I'll grab you and tear off your clothes and have my way with you before you can scream for help?" She sighed, said, "Fat chance," and shook off the mental image.

Hearing the commotion downstairs, Cole planed away a sixteenth of an inch too much wood, swore and laid aside his plane. Whatever the hell she was doing down there, she obviously didn't need help, else she would've asked for it. Yeah, right.

He was tempted to go see what the devil she was up to, but even more determined to mind his own business. He didn't understand women. Never had, never would. And Marty Owens was in a class by herself.

He waited until he'd swept up shavings and sawdust before he headed downstairs. There was barely enough room to stand.

She confronted him at the foot of the stairs, hands on her hips. "I didn't move it all by myself—a neighbor helped."

Cole was forced to step over a stack of desk drawers. "Are you out of your mind?" he demanded.

"Well, I don't know. What's your diagnosis?"

Her tone was suspiciously reasonable, her eyes suspiciously glittery. Her small, rounded chin jutted out as if daring him to take a swing at her.

As if he would. As if he would ever hit a woman, no matter what the provocation. "You want my diagnosis? Clinically speaking, I think you're scared out of your gourd. I think you're trying to put yourself in a position where backing out's not an option. How'm I doing so far?"

"I hired you as a builder, not a shrink. Is that trash? Give it to me, I'll take it out." After snapping out orders like a small female general, she reached for the bag.

He stepped back and attempted to stare her down. "Your jaw's about to snap out of alignment."

"Just give me the damn trash bag!"

So he handed it over. "Tie your shoelace before you trip."

She took a deep breath, drawing his attention to her upper assets, which were—in his estimation, at least—just about perfect.

She poked the bag back at him. "Then you do it!" Normally her complexion was parchment pale, but now twin splotches of color bloomed on her cheeks. The tip of her nose was pink, and her eyes—

Oh, hell, they were starting to leak again.

He dropped the sack of sawdust and shavings, stepped over two desk drawers, endangering the contents, and before the first tear splashed down he had her safely in his arms. "Hey, it's no big deal, honey. Whoa, now, don't cry. Rainy days are made for doing stuff you don't ordinarily have time for, like rearranging furniture. I knew this woman once who—"

"I don't want to know about your d-damn women," she sobbed, her voice muffled against his shirt.

He was filthy—covered in sawdust, but that didn't keep him from holding her while he made those noises men make when they feel about as useful as tits on a male dog.

"This is twice," she sobbed. "Th—that's a record."

He hadn't the least idea what she was talking about, not that it mattered.

Her hair tickled his chin even as her soft, warm body wriggled closer. If ever a woman needed holding, this one did. He wouldn't even claim any merit badges for taking on the job, because some jobs were their own reward.

"Shh, it's all right, honey. Good idea, in fact."

"What's good about it?"

Feeling her fingers at his waistband, he instinctively sucked in his breath. She was pulling out his shirttail? To do what? *To get to what?*

To use it as a handkerchief.

"I'll wash it," she promised, her elbows poking him in the chest as she tugged his flannel shirttail up to her face to dry her tears.

Without releasing her, he shifted his hips to one side in an effort to hide his body's enthusiastic reaction. Talk about a trial by fire!

He made a few more of the only kind of noises a man can make when his brain skips out leaving no forwarding address.

When she dropped his shirttail and wrapped both arms around his waist, pulling him into alignment again, he closed his eyes and prayed for patience. Forbearance. Maybe sainthood.

"Whoa—that is, uh—why don't I take that trash out while you, uh—find a place to sit down. Then, when I come back I'll make us some coffee and we can talk about what you're planning to do in here. How's that sound?"

He didn't wait for an answer, but gently pried her arms from around his waist. It was either put some distance between them—a couple of continents should do it—or lower her onto the nearest flat surface and let nature take its course.

She sucked in a shaky breath and stepped back. And then, damn if she didn't smile at him. Red eyes, pink nose, wet cheeks and all, it was that smile that cut through all the scars that had built up over the years, making him think thoughts he had absolutely no business thinking.

And not just of sex, either.

So he grabbed the sack of trash and fled.

Talk about cutting off your nose to spite your face— she'd had some crazy idea that by moving out what had to go out and moving in what had to come in she could get ahead of schedule and put an end to all the second thoughts that were driving her batty. The deeper she got into this mess she'd created, the harder it was to extricate herself.

Marty shoved aside the sofa cushions and snatched her coat from the closet. She scrambled around and found a rain hat that was as old as dirt and probably no longer waterproof, but then, it hadn't actually started raining yet. She jammed it on her head, snatched her purse and left. She'd better get in the last dog-walk because later was looking less and less likely.

The car started on the second try, just as Cole came around the corner of the house. He called out and waved his arms. Marty pretended not to see or hear. She didn't want to talk to him now, she really didn't. So she backed over her bulb bed to get around his truck, and just as she pulled out onto the street, the first few spatters of rain struck the windshield.

* * *

Cole watched the white minivan disappear around the corner. He was tempted to follow her. If she needed provisions before the weather closed in, she should have said so. If she wanted to get in a second dog-walk before things got too messy, then she should have told him, dammit, and he'd have gone with her.

Had she forgotten about that Mercedes?

Oh, hell, she didn't need him. If nothing else, she'd proved that much with this morning's exercise. For all he knew, she tore up her house and shifted all her furniture whenever the notion struck her. What did he know about women, anyway? Paula, the spoiled daughter of a construction worker who'd been canny enough—or maybe just crooked enough—to make millions, might have been born with a stainless steel spoon in her mouth, but she'd quickly adapted to sterling.

As for his mother, Aurelia Stevens had been a piano teacher who had never gotten over her dream of being a concert pianist. Cole had watched her grow old, staring out the window day after day, year after year, as one or another tin-eared kid who would rather be outdoors playing ball, abused her precious baby grand.

Both Cole and his father, a security guard with a serious drinking problem who'd had trouble holding a job, had saved for years to buy her that piano. That was one of the reasons it had got to him when Paula had decided she needed a Steinway to fill the corner of what she called her drawing room. She didn't even like music, much less play. She'd majored in cheerleading. Rah, rah, rah...

Back to Marty, he told himself as a soft freezing mist dampened his face. Follow her or get back to work?

He settled for hauling all the furniture he could handle single-handedly upstairs and stashing it in the larger of the two bedrooms, the one she planned to use as a living room. The sofa would have to wait. Maybe once the weather let up he could get Bob Ed to lend him a hand in exchange for the windows he'd installed.

That done, he worked on fitting the cabinet doors, marking and chiseling out for the hinges. Some time later he glanced at the clock. It wasn't as late as it looked, but she'd already been gone nearly two hours. Something between sleet and frozen rain fell steadily, although judging from the few cars that passed by, nothing was sticking to the streets. The temperature still hovered a few degrees above freezing.

At three, he called Bob Ed and asked him to check on the boat. "I left a leeward port open a crack for fresh air. Would you mind closing it? And while you're there, how about listening to be sure the bilge pump's not running. The timer's been giving me some trouble lately. Oh, and I probably won't make it back tonight."

By the time he heard Marty pull into the driveway, Cole had the lower doors ready to hang. He'd tried working on the drawers, but had given it up. Everything was a mess, himself included. His concentration was shot. Damn, it was none of his business where she went, or who she spent her time with.

So how come it felt like his business?

He went downstairs, just as she came in through the front door, bringing with her a waft of cold, wet air. Shaking moisture from her coat and stripping off the ugliest hat he'd ever seen, she stopped dead in her tracks.

"How come you're still here? I thought you'd leave early today on account of the weather." She looked around slowly. "And where's all my furniture?"

"Most of it's upstairs. Your shoes are wet, better take

'em off before you catch cold." The legs of her pants were wet, too, but he wasn't about to go there.

"I'm numb. It's freezing outside!"

She shivered and rubbed her hands together, and Cole forgot all the things he'd intended to say about having a plan and sticking to it, about not going off half-cocked, and especially about not going off without telling him where she was headed and when she expected to return.

"You wouldn't believe the day I've had," she said, shaking her head.

The hat had left her hair plastered to her forehead and frizzed out on the ends. On her, it looked…cute.

"Tell me there's coffee in the pot."

He cleared his throat. "Which part of your day wouldn't I believe? The part where the first elephant invaded your living room, or the part where—"

"Oh, hush up." She tossed her wet coat toward the bench, where he'd stacked the contents of her coffee table before toting the table upstairs. "I haven't eaten a bite in ages, so don't talk to me, okay? I'm mean as a junkyard dog when I'm hungry."

A slow grin spread across his face. "Yeah, I believe you," he said as he followed her into the kitchen and waited for her reaction to the two bookcases he'd cut down while she was gone. All four sections.

Compared with bringing her flowers or candy, it hardly rated. As he waited for some sign of approval, he realized with a degree of alarm just how much her approval meant to him.

Trouble was, there was no easy way he could back off at this stage.

Eleven

So then Cole had to explain how he'd called the marina and left orders to secure the *Time Out,* and how he'd stuck around because he'd been worried about her, and how as long as he was here, he'd figured he might as well accomplish something.

"Accomplish something! You've done all this—?" She waved her hands around the room, where the only alien pieces were the bookshelves. "My God, in—what, two hours?"

"More like four. I'd have had the rest of them done and moved into the living room, ready for you to start stocking with books, if you'd been any later." The truth was, he'd been about ready to go out and beat the bushes looking for her. Muddy Landing wasn't all that big. He figured he could cover it in less than an hour as long as he didn't mind breaking a few speed laws.

And as long as she'd stayed in town.

She could have been anywhere. She could've taken a notion to drive up to Chesapeake with her nutty redheaded friend. To say Marty was maddening didn't begin to describe how she frustrated him, but it was a start.

She refused to look at him. Marty was in no mood to be fussed at. Leaning back, elbows braced on the table, she toe-heeled off her wet shoes. Then, groaning, she bent over and pulled off her socks. Her feet were bluish white, her toes red.

"You walked the dog, didn't you."

Whether or not he meant it as an accusation, that's the way she took it.

"So? I agreed to two walks a day. The times weren't specified." She ran her fingers through her hair and frowned down at the wet ends. "That dumb dog thinks rules don't count on rainy days. Either that or he's already forgotten everything you taught him." Propping one foot on her knee, she tried to thaw it out with massage.

"I didn't teach Mutt, I taught you!"

Dropping her foot to the floor, she glared at him. "Okay, so *I'm* the one who forgot. Or maybe I didn't sleep in the right motel!" When he continued to stare at her as if she'd lost her mind—there were no guarantees on that score—she said glumly, "That TV ad—you know. You don't need any fancy degrees as long as you stay in the right motel? Hotel? Whatever."

And then she sneezed twice in quick succession.

He scooped her up in his arms before she could do more than squawk in protest. Balancing her on an upraised knee, he managed to switch on the coffeemaker with one hand, and then he headed upstairs. "You're the one who started this mess," he growled. "Three guesses who'll get blamed if you don't meet your deadline. You want to catch pneumonia?"

"You don't catch pneumonia from wet feet, you catch it from—"

"From bugs! I know that, dammit! Maybe I didn't sleep in the right hotel, but at least I know that a hot bath, dry warm clothes, and something hot to drink won't hurt you, and it might even help. You got any whiskey?"

If it hadn't sounded so good—if he hadn't felt so good—Marty might have put up more of a fight, but she was so tired and so cold. She'd picked up a neighbor whose car wouldn't start and taken her to the library and then made two more stops. What are neighbors for?

"Under the toaster. I mean, under the counter where the toaster sits. It's in a jar, not a bottle."

Upstairs in the bathroom, he set her on her feet with orders to strip. Then he closed the valve and turned on the water, adjusting it until he was evidently satisfied it was hot enough to kill any cold germs.

"You need any help?" he demanded when she just stood there like a lamppost with the bulb burned out.

Steam rose from the tub, quickly clouding the mirror in the chilly room. When she pulled the sweater off and dropped it on the floor, he picked it up and draped it over his arm.

A tidy man? Would wonders never cease?

"What about stuff women always put in the water? You use anything like that?"

She glanced at the jar of bath salts. She used it not for the scent—well, partially for that, but mostly because it cut down on rings in the tub. Following her glance, he reached for the jar and before she could stop him, dumped half the contents into the steaming water.

"Too much," she protested. "That's way, way too much!"

"Too late," he mimicked. "Way, way too late. You should've told me."

"You should have given me time! By the way, did I tell you you're fired?" Her teeth were chattering, and not just from cold. Heat pumps were no match for this kind of weather, but whoever heard of a bathroom fireplace?

He shook his head. "Get in the tub, Marty. I'll bring you something to put on."

"Didn't you hear me? You're fired."

"Right. I'll pack up my tools and leave just as soon as I finish your new kitchen."

"Just stop being so damn reasonable, will you?"

"Just finish getting undressed and hit the tub, will you?"

She took a deep, shuddering breath, willing herself not to bawl. Again. Caution: streaky-haired men with sexy bodies can be hazardous to your health. The FDA or somebody ought to stamp his side with a purple warning to that effect.

"You need help?"

"Thank you, you've done quite enough," she said stiffly.

"Then hop to it."

"As soon as you leave," she said. Her jeans were wet from the thighs down. She had goose bumps on her goose bumps, but she refused to strip naked with him standing there leering at her.

Okay, so maybe he wasn't leering, but he was still here, and she had no intention of—

With a sigh that reeked of strained patience, he shut off the water just as it reached the overflow drain. "Marty, I'm trying to help you here, but you're not making it easy."

"Then leave. Go somewhere else, I don't care where, just leave before I'm forced to throw you out."

He opened his mouth to speak and obviously thought better of it. Shaking his head, he left, taking her sweater with him, leaving behind the faint scent of fresh-cut lumber and a cedar-citrus aftershave that cut through her vanilla-scented, grocery-store-brand bath salts.

Once the door closed behind him, she wasted no time in stepping out of her clothes and testing the water with one foot. It was perfect.

Well, damn. Along with everything else, he knew how to draw a lady's bath.

She eased herself under the deliciously hot water up to her neck and released a sigh of perfect contentment. All right, maybe not perfect, but close enough. She'd just have to remember to be extra careful getting out, because the tub would be slick as black ice.

Dunking her hair, she felt along the ledge for her shampoo. Normally she shampooed under the shower, but today she just didn't care. She was torn between wanting to get out and confront him in a slam-bang showdown and wanting to hide out here where it was deliciously warm.

By the time she had rinsed away the suds and opened her eyes again, Cole was seated on the stool where she sat to clip her toenails. He held out a hand towel.

"You ready to dry your face?"

She snatched it, blotted her stinging eyes and glared at him. "I told you, you're fired. Go home. Go anywhere, I don't care where, just get out of my house."

"Did I tell you I worked as a lifeguard a couple of summers back when I was in school?"

"Fine. Throw me a life ring and then get out." She crossed her arms over her chest, leaving the rest of her body vulnerable. The water was slightly cloudy, but it was hardly opaque. "Cole, what are you trying to do? I take back your firing, if that's what you want."

He shook his head. Seated on an ivory enameled stool with his knees spread apart and his big feet planted on her pink and white crocheted rug, he should have looked ludicrous. Instead, he looked…

The bath water that had started to cool off seemed suddenly too hot to bear.

He said, "Are you finished? I'll help you out so you don't slip. I should've read the instructions on that bath stuff before I dumped it in."

"You're not going to leave, are you." If she sounded resigned, it was because she knew what was going to happen next. Knew it as well as she knew she was in trouble way over her head. Life rings weren't going to help.

She wet the hand towel and draped it over her breasts. With one hand she shielded her groin from view, with the other hand she reached for his. If she slipped and fell, maybe she'd simply lie there and drown. At least the wake would be interesting, with people setting casseroles and cupcakes on bookshelves and looking for a chair where they could sit and talk about how poor Marty Owens had finally flipped her ever-loving lid.

He'd turned his head when she stood, but the moment both her feet were safely out of the tub he enveloped her in a bath towel. As the water gurgled down the drain, he dropped another towel over her hair and gave it a rub or two.

"You use a drier?" he asked.

She clutched the bath towel around her, shivering, but not from cold. She was warm to the bone. Warm and needy and standing too close to temptation.

And if that wasn't a song title, it should be.

He gave her hair another rub and then started blotting her arms, his face so close she could see the black pupils in those tarnished brass eyes. Pupils that seemed to expand even as she watched. She stopped breathing. So did he. Slowly, she lifted her arms around his neck. When the towel slipped from her shoulders, neither of them noticed.

Under his dark flannel shirt he wore a tee that looked startlingly white against the tanned skin of his throat. She kissed the hollow where a pulse was beating in time with her own racing heart.

"Well, are you going to kiss me, or not?" she asked. Ever the realist, she recognized the inevitable and lifted her face to his.

He was. He did.

Oh, my mercy, how he did.

While his tongue invaded her mouth, his hands slowly slid down her sides, fingertips teasing the sides of her breasts. Then his hands closed over her hipbones and he moved her back and forth, tantalizing her with the hard ridge that thrust against her belly.

When she nibbled the tip of his tongue and then sucked on it, his fingers bit almost painfully into her waist. By the time she broke away from the kiss—only because she had to breathe—his face was flushed, his eyes black with excitement.

She knew the signs, oh, yes. She'd read all about it. She'd just never before seen it, at least not to this extent. After two husbands, that was probably something of a record. Sasha had tried to tell her there was a whole world out there, just waiting to be explored.

"Bed?" he panted.

"Please. I have a box of—"

"Good," he said. "A big box?"

They made it to the bedroom, and she was thankful for all those early years when she'd made her bed to perfection each morning. He carried her past the jumble of furniture, peeled back the neat covers and lowered her to the mattress. And then, while she watched, he stripped off his clothes in what had to be record time.

"I'll go slow," he said, his voice thick, almost grim.

"Don't."

She held up her arms, but instead of taking her invitation, he knelt beside her, his breathing audible even over the slithery sound of sleet pelting the windows.

His gaze was as hot as molten steel as it led the way, followed by his hands, and then his lips. He kissed her eyelid, her ears and her nose. His lips moved down her throat, lingering on that spot that drove her wild.

How could he know?

When he reached her breasts, he cupped them, squeezing them gently, then used his thumbs, his teeth and his tongue on the nipples to drive her totally wild.

Only at that point, she didn't yet know what wild was. Not until he came up on his knees again and she caught a glimpse of...

Oh, my. The word *magnificent* came to mind. So did all those pop-ups on her computer, and the magazine articles she'd scoffed at, believing them to be fiction, if not outright fantasy.

When he buried his face in her quivering belly and then moved south, all hope of rational thought disappeared. In blind supplication she lifted her hips and whimpered,

"Please…" She wanted him inside her while she was still conscious. Already she was feeling rainbows—

Not seeing them, but *feeling* them!

She tugged at his ears, and then his hair, and then her fingers raked over his slick shoulders, dragging him up to where she wanted him. "Please," she begged.

"Give me a minute," he said hoarsely.

Never had a minute seemed so endless, while he ripped open a packet and covered himself. She would have loved to do it for him—only she was no expert and this was no time to further her education.

He kissed her again, tasting of mint, coffee and musk. On his knees and one elbow, he guided himself in place, thrust once and was still.

Hurry, hurry, she wanted to scream when a year passed and he didn't move again. And then he did move, tracing the hills and valleys of her body, burying his face between her breasts, stroking her with his tongue. Utterly boneless, she melted as he suckled her nipples.

Somehow, their positions reversed, and he guided her eager hands down his taut body, lingering where he wanted her attention.

And then it was her turn…again. All too soon she caught her breath—caught it again—forgetting each time to exhale. He thrust faster, harder—she cried out.

He whispered her name, his voice sounding as if he were in pain.

Long moments later she felt a drift of cool air on her back when he rolled over onto his side, taking her with him. His eyes were closed. His skin was slick with sweat, and he was breathing as if he'd just run a three-minute mile.

As echoes of her first truly magnificent orgasm slowly faded, Marty took the opportunity to stare wonderingly at his face—at the laugh lines and the squint lines, and those deliciously long, dark lashes.

This is the face of the man I love, she thought, stunned by the realization.

They must have slept, because the next thing he knew the phone was ringing. It was still in Marty's old bedroom, waiting for a phone jack to be installed in the room where they now slept.

Cole rolled over onto his back when he felt her leave. He squinted at the wristwatch that was all he was wearing at the moment.

A little after half-past four—a.m. or p.m.? Must be p.m., judging from the light outside. Still gray, but not completely dark.

He considered getting up, but lacked the energy. Without intentionally eavesdropping he heard her say, "Oh, he's great. Mmm-hmm, twice already today."

Twice, hell. That near miss downstairs didn't count.

"Well, you don't have to do that—really, I enjoyed it."

Yeah, me, too, he thought, satisfaction oozing from his pores.

He must have dozed. Hearing her opening a dresser drawer, he forced himself to sit up. "Problem?" he asked.

"What? Oh, no—nothing like that." She took out a set of underwear and then shook out a sweater, frowned at it and exchanged it for another one.

He continued to watch her in the mirror. "You want to come back to bed?"

Without looking at him, she shook her head. How come,

he wondered, women considered bed-head a bad thing? On her it looked great. Soft and sexy and a little wild.

"You want to go downstairs and roll those bookshelves into the living room?"

"Mmm-hmm," she said.

She was wrapped in a quilt that had been on the foot of the bed. Sooner or later she was going to have to look at him. The sex had been too good to ignore.

But Marty was…well, she was Marty. He had a feeling she'd been through almost as long a dry spell as he had. She would come to terms with it in her own sweet time. Meanwhile, he could afford to wait. She still hadn't told him who'd called…not that it was any of his business.

It snowed for about twenty minutes just after dark. They stood at the window and watched it swirl around the street-light. Cole's arm was around her shoulders as if it had every right to be there.

Marty wanted to believe it did, but she was too much a realist. Regardless of what the constitution said, not all men were created equal. At least, not where sex was concerned. Sex with Alan had been…well, not exactly boring, but limited, to say the least. With Beau, it had been exciting at first, but afterward she'd always felt as if the bus had come and gone, and she'd missed it. She'd never complained, knowing there'd be another bus a few days later, but she'd missed most of those, too.

With Cole…

She sighed. "I forgot about supper."

"Anything in the freezer? I doubt that anything's open tonight. There's no traffic."

Half an hour later they had shared freezer pizza with

dabs of this and that from the refrigerator. She had drawn the line at horseradish on her half. After a call from Faylene, reminding her of Bob Ed's birthday party tomorrow night, they had moved a few more of the bookcases into the living room.

Now Marty was torn between standing in the doorway looking at them and telling herself it really was going to happen, and grabbing Cole and dragging him upstairs to bed. Upstairs wasn't even a priority. Anywhere would do. The table…the living room rug…

Cole offered to bring down her boxes of books, but she explained that before she could even think about stocking her shelves she needed to paint the walls and do a final cleaning. "Sasha has this crazy idea—"

"Red walls, right?"

"Three shades of red. I'm probably going to compromise and do all four walls in the palest shade of peach. That's warm enough for a northern exposure, don't you think?"

He stood there looking both sexy and thoughtful in his jeans and navy flannel shirt with only a hint of sawdust around the collar. He had showered and now he smelled of her soap, but he hadn't taken time to shave. She was tempted to stroke his bristly jaw, but she knew better than to touch him again. This was one case where the hair of the dog didn't count.

"The Hallets are back," she said. "That's who called, so no more dog-walking."

"I thought you had another week."

"Everybody got sick, so they cut the cruise short. Big disappointment." She was grinning. "So…how about if I help you hang the cabinet doors?"

"How about if you help me cut down the last two bookshelves?" he countered.

"Deal," she said, and held up a hand, palm outward.

He slapped it with his, and his fingers threatened to interweave with hers, but he dropped his hand. "Deal," he said softly.

Evidently, she wasn't the only one who knew better than to tempt fate.

Twelve

Feeling absurdly self-conscious for a woman of thirty-seven—a woman who had been married twice—Marty pulled on her third outfit, a pink wool turtleneck and maroon slacks. She checked her image in the dresser mirror and decided it would have to do. Her bed was piled with outfits she had tried on and discarded, which was just as well, because now she could look at her bed and think of what she needed to do instead of what she'd already done.

Yesterday. And again last night. Twice!

Cole had woken early and driven back to the marina to check on his boat and collect a few clean clothes. She'd woken up when she'd heard his truck drive off and had sat there for several minutes reliving every kiss, every embrace, every tingling, bone-melting climax.

That was it? she'd thought, stunned. He was leaving? At six-oh-whatever in the morning? Her eyes wouldn't focus well enough to tell the exact time, but thinking she might never see him again, she'd been devastated. She had forced herself to get up, shower and dress. Life went on. If she hadn't learned that lesson after Alan and Beau, she'd darn well better learn it now…after Cole.

She'd just been touching her lashes with mascara when she'd heard him drive up again. Mascara! At seven-twenty in the morning!

You have flat out lost it, lady, she'd told herself.

As it turned out, he had stopped by the grocery store on the way back, bringing enough provisions to last an entire platoon a week.

"Are you *that* hungry?" she'd demanded. Relief came out sounding like irritation…which was probably just as well.

Without answering, he waggled his eyebrows and grinned.

Not a word about last night. Not a word about stealing her heart, her body, and anything else she had of value.

Together, they had worked all day, taking time out only to make sandwiches. At five she had come upstairs to shower and start getting ready for the birthday party, while he'd continued to rearrange shelves, leaving space to work around them to repaint her walls.

Once he'd heard the shower cut off, he had joined her upstairs. "Casual?" he'd asked, poking his head into the bedroom.

"Definitely."

"Good. Otherwise, I'd have had to rush up to Virginia Beach and get my tux out of storage."

He had whistled while he showered, shaved and dressed, taking half the time it had taken her just to decide on what to wear to Bob Ed's party. While she'd stood in front of the mirror trying to do something with her hair, he had leaned in the doorway, again offering advice. She'd finally run him downstairs, but her heart had done cartwheels. If he'd so much as touched her, they'd have ended up back in bed.

All day long, while they'd whacked off and nailed on end boards in the garage and moved shelves into the house, she'd felt as self-conscious as a fourteen-year-old on her first date. That unsure of herself—which was absurd in a woman of her age. An experienced adult who'd had two husbands. You'd think they'd done something bizarre and a little kinky instead of just making love—

Not making love. Having sex. Big, big difference, she reminded herself sternly as she fastened a pair of gold hoops on her ears.

"Do we need to take anything? Beer? Wine? Food?" Cole called upstairs just as she started down.

"Lord, no. He'd be highly insulted. One of his clients has a brewery and another one has a barbecue catering service. That'll give you an idea of what the menu will be tonight." She joined him in the hall, glancing at her watch. Being a Virgo, she was always punctual, but that was before time had stopped three times during the night.

"I thought it was stewed Canada goose with all the trimmings," he murmured, leaning over to inhale the scent of shampoo, soap and jasmine-scented body lotion.

He even claimed to be addicted to her coconut-flavored lip balm.

"That's only the beginning," she said breathlessly as she slid her arms into the sleeves of her warmest coat. She was about to tell him he looked good—and oh, my mercy, he did!—when he beat her to the punch.

"You look beautiful, Marty. I like what you've done to your hair."

She had twisted it into a knot, anchored it with a fancy craft-show comb, and pulled out a few tendrils to curl at the sides. Ordinarily, she settled for a scrunchy. She could feel her face reddening.

Making a big deal out of checking her purse for necessary items, she thanked him.

Yesterday's sleety rain was now only a damp memory. Streaks of gold and lavender brightened the western sky. To the east, the Hamburger Shanty's neon sign cast a cheerful glow against the fast-disappearing storm clouds. Faylene swore that in all the years she'd known Bob Ed, it had never rained on one of his parties.

Marty had a feeling it could be raining buffaloes and she wouldn't notice. "Your car, mine, or both?" she asked. Code for *Will you be coming back here tonight, or are you moving back aboard your boat now that the weather's let up?*

"Mine—if that's all right with you?"

A semi-self-conscious silence prevailed the rest of the way to the marina. Halfway there, Cole put on a CD. This time instead of Chopin, it was classical guitar. It could have been Spike Jones and his City Slickers and it wouldn't have made a speck of difference. Any music shared was romantic music.

The parking area was jam-packed with vehicles of all descriptions. Sasha's red convertible was parked close to the wharf. She had evidently come early to help with the preparations, although she knew better than to offer Bob Ed any decorating advice. Faylene still laughed about the time Sasha had made him a centerpiece using port and starboard running lights, a small anchor and three fat candles.

Cole found a place down near the end of the wharf, near his own boat. "Man, I had no idea it was this big a deal," he murmured as he helped her from the truck, taking her arm and leading her toward the big, unpainted building that served the guide as both home and office.

Marty hugged his arm to her side. "It might not look like it, but Bob Ed's place is famous all up and down the coast. His clients like to believe it's their own private discovery— this little hole-in-the-wall marina just off the beaten track." They dodged a puddle, necessitating a bumping of hips and shoulders. He smiled down at her, causing her heart to skip a beat, and she quickly looked away. Tonight was going to be tricky. One look and Sasha would know exactly what had happened. The woman had the internal radar of a bat.

Every window was lighted, guests spilled out along the wharf on both sides, and from the sound—and the smells— the party was well underway. They had just sidled between two pickup trucks, both bristling with rod holders, when she happened to catch sight of a familiar car. She stopped dead in her tracks and stared.

"Is that what I think it is?"

It was a gray Mercedes, far from new, but in excellent condition. Among all the SUVs and pickups, it stuck out like a sore thumb.

"Yep. Coincidence?" Cole murmured. "I don't think so." He moved around to check the license plate. "This should be interesting."

It was all the excuse she needed to hang on to his arm, tucking her hand against his side to feel his comforting warmth. "Look, I probably made too big a deal of the whole thing," she said. "Otherwise, whoever it is wouldn't be right out here where anyone could spot him."

"He was right out in plain sight when he was following you. He didn't mind being seen when he parked in your neighbor's driveway."

"So he's a gutsy stalker." She attempted a carefree laugh, but it wasn't very convincing. "Or maybe he's new at it. Maybe he's just got a learner's permit."

And then someone said, "Excuse me," and they stepped back to allow one of the locals to pass. He was carrying a washtub filled with ice.

"Well, hey there, Miss Marty. My wife says when you going to get your bookstore open again?"

Her wariness faded. "Oh, hi, James. Tell her soon, I hope." Looking back at Cole, she murmured, "It occurred to me that I'll need to advertise. Mail out cards or buy radio time. Maybe even a trailer on the local weather station."

By then they'd reached the door, which was propped open. They were immediately enveloped in a noisy, good-natured crowd, and Marty forgot about both advertising and her wacky stalker. Snatches of string music could be heard over the sound of laughter and dozens of voices all trying to be heard. The mingled scent of hickory barbecue and something gamier mingled with Brut, Old Spice and Eau de Whatever.

Someone yelled, "Marty, you're the expert. Tell this here dumbhead that Clive Cussler's been diving around these parts for years."

"Expert on popular fiction, maybe, but not on diving. But yes, actually, I think he has."   .

A strident voice yelled, "The potatoes is done!"

Someone else said, "We got enough Texas Pete?"

"Oh, lawsy, I lost an earring in the stew pot!"

As a dozen conversations swirled around her, Sasha sidled

over and whispered in her ear, "Oh, honey, do I have a hot prospect for Lily! He's right over there, talking to the sheriff." On social occasions, local law enforcement overlooked minor infractions of certain laws. Tonight was obviously one of those occasions, as the man in question was holding a glass of clear liquid. Chances were, it wasn't vodka.

Faylene joined them. "Gus and Cassie, whaddya think? Her boobs and his beer belly ought to be a fit. Picture it."

Marty did. She giggled.

Sasha said, "The mind boggles."

From several feet away, Cole winked at her. He'd been buttonholed by old Miss Katie, a retired schoolteacher who considered anyone under the age of fifty to still have a few things to learn. She was probably right, Marty thought ruefully. About some of us, at least.

The party was in full swing by the time Marty broke away more than an hour later. Several people had stepped outside for a breath of cool air, among them an attractive middle-aged man wearing flannel and tweed and smoking a pipe. Probably a college professor, she thought. He didn't look like a hunter or fisherman—but who ever knew?

She watched idly as he stepped down from the wharf and made his way past two trucks and an SUV. A moment later she saw a light come on as he opened the door of the Mercedes. Without taking time to think, she hopped down and followed. Just as she reached him, he closed the car door and turned away, holding what looked like a tobacco pouch.

"Stop right there," she commanded.

He stopped. He stared. In the cold green glow of the mercury-vapor security light, she could almost believe his face reddened, but she could have been mistaken.

"Ms. Owens?" he said.

"Have you been following me?" While she waited for a denial, she tried to think of a way to make him confess. How did they do it in books? Threats? Torture? Both out of the question—but he was the one, all right. She knew it.

Proving it was another matter. "Just tell me this—why is it that you turn up everywhere I go? Even here." All right, so he'd been here when she'd arrived; that was a minor technicality.

He tucked the pouch in the pocket of his tweed jacket and she caught a hint of vanilla-scented pipe tobacco.

"Ms. Owens, do you have any sisters?"

Puzzled, she tilted her head. "Sisters? Look, whoever you are, I'm not answering any questions until you tell me what's going on."

Only a few feet separated them in the crowded parking area. The man didn't look all that dangerous—she might even be able to take him in a fair fight. But she'd rather not put it to the test. Her knowledge of martial arts had come from reading suspense and watching Jackie Chan.

"I do," he said, sounding almost resigned.

"You do what?" That's right, she thought—throw me off balance.

"Have a sister. Her name is Marissa Owens and she lives outside Culpepper. Kenyon Farms—at least it used to be a farm. All that's left is the house and one empty stable. You might know the place."

Oh, my God. She did. Beau had taken her there just once, right after they'd been married. His mother, who had not attended the wedding, had been frigidly polite throughout the brief visit.

"Then you're…"

"Beau's uncle, James Merchison. I'm truly sorry if I've frightened you. That was never my intention, but when my sister heard I was headed down to Hobe Sound, she asked me to lay over here long enough to find out if you still had any of the things Beau took from home. They're family pieces, you know. We'd be more than willing to buy them back."

"Then why didn't you come right out and ask me?"

"I should have, but I didn't know what to ask. It's embarrassing to be put in the position of accusing someone who was once family of—well, I suppose it could be called receiving stolen goods."

Marty took a deep breath and expelled it in a sharp huff. He looked so apologetic that she was inclined to forgive him, but not before she told him exactly what a piece of work his nephew was.

"Do you know he even stole my wedding ring? Not that it was all that valuable—it definitely wasn't a family heirloom, because I was with him when we picked it out. He told me he was going to have it checked to be sure none of the stones were loose, and then he claimed the jeweler lost it." She glanced down at her bare finger. "As for the paintings he claimed his mother gave him because she didn't have room to hang them, they hung on our walls for—oh, maybe five months. He claimed he was going to have them appraised for insurance purposes. I never saw them again."

They were still comparing notes on the lying, gambling-addicted wretch she'd had the misfortune to marry when Cole found her. His eyes narrowed as he took possession of her arm.

"Is there a problem here?"

Marty introduced the two men. The older man said, "Merchison, Saunders, Vessels and Wilson, Attorneys at Law."

"Then I guess I don't have to tell you what you've been doing is probably actionable," Cole said evenly.

"It was personal. I've apologized and explained to the lady."

"He has, Cole, and I understand. Really, I do." She patted James Merchison on the hand. "If I were you and I were looking for Beau, I'd cruise on up to Atlantic City. Or anywhere there's gambling."

The three of them rejoined the party in time to fill paper plates with everything from stewed goose and dumplings to barbecue, to grilled tuna and crab cakes. Beverages ranged from soft drinks to beer to gallon jugs of white liquor of the no-questions-asked variety.

While Cole worked his way closer to the musicians, Marty cornered Faylene to compliment her on her new hairstyle, which was more Farrah Faucett than Dolly Parton.

"Law heppus, if this wind don't let up, I'm gonna get me one o' them WeedEater cuts. Whatcha think of that feller over there with the Mercedes for Miss Lily? She's some taller, but some men like that in a woman."

It was long past midnight when they got home. Neither of them questioned the fact that Cole would be spending the night there; otherwise he'd have suggested that they drive separately. For the past few hours they had mingled, sometimes separately, sometimes together. Cole had wandered over to talk to the musicians, but even across the room she'd felt his gaze return to her again and again, his eyes glowing with a message she was almost afraid to interpret for fear she'd get it wrong.

Looking around her house now as she shed her coat, she shook her head. "It still comes as a shock when I see the chaos. Can you believe I used to be compulsively neat?"

"Yeah, I can believe it."

His smile held sympathy and more understanding than she was ready to accept.

"You want a nightcap?"

"After that feast? I don't think so."

"I don't, either."

And then neither of them could think of anything to say. Marty reminded herself that she'd lived with the man—well, practically lived with him—for a week. They had shared meals and dog-walks and shopping; she had introduced him to her friends, argued with him and even fired him.

She had made love to him, for heaven's sake.

So why was she acting like an idiot? Why was she quaking inside? Was she afraid he was going to tell her goodnight and drive all the way back to the marina?

"Look, do you want to go to bed, or not?" she blurted. "With me, I mean. You can always sleep on the sofa. It's a mess in there, but I can give you a pillow and a blanket and—"

He hushed her with a finger over her lips. His eyes were laughing. At her, or with her?

Oh, Lord, you'd think she'd eventually learn, wouldn't you?

Upstairs, Cole helped her hang up the clothing she'd left scattered across the bed. Then he undressed her, carefully easing her turtleneck sweater over her head.

"Sorry I messed up your hair. It looked pretty, but I like it the way you usually wear it, too." He was so close she could feel the heat of his body through the navy flannel and whatever he wore under it.

When he stood her up again and unbuttoned the waistband of her slacks she noticed how unsteady his hands were. "You don't have to do this," she whispered. Whispered because she couldn't seem to breathe properly.

"Yeah, I do. Measure twice, cut once. It's an old carpenter's saying."

She clutched his shoulder and stepped out of her slacks. "You're not all that old," she teased, but she knew what he meant. The evidence was…well, evident. Aroused all the way up to his belt buckle, he was taking his time with the preliminaries, doing his best not to rush.

His own clothes came off quickly, though. Khaki, flannel and cotton knit, tossed at a chair, half of it falling to the floor. Marty pulled out her box of condoms and took one—and then another one. And then a third. Just in case. Sooner or later they were going to have to talk.

Or not.

Color stained his angular cheeks. His hands trembled, but there was nothing at all hurried or unsure about his kisses. Slowly, he explored her mouth, his tongue dueling with hers, then thrusting in a seductive promise of things to come. He kissed her eyelids, her ears, suckling the lobes. The moment his lips found that sensitive place at the side of her throat, she sucked in her breath, goose bumps racing in waves down her flanks.

"I…can't…wait," she managed to whisper when his tongue traced a pattern around her nipple. While her fists flailed the sheets and her head moved from side to side on the pillow, he proceeded to drive her wild, first with his hands, then with his lips and his tongue.

"I need you...now!" she whispered fiercely. If he would just come inside her and ease this intolerable ache he'd created, then she might survive. Otherwise, there were no guarantees.

"You don't know how much I've wanted this," he said in a raspy voice, nipping her belly with soft ferocity. "I've waited all night—all day—all week."

He aligned her underneath him. As if they'd done it a thousand times, her toes pushed against his, then her knees lifted to clasp his hips and she breathed in the clean musky scent of his body. She felt the tip of him move intimately against her.

He hesitated. "Tell me what you want," he said, lifting his head so that he could watch her reaction.

She didn't know whether to laugh or cry. After years of thinking of herself as lukewarm in matters pertaining to sex, in a single night this man had turned her into a woman she didn't even recognize. A woman who was daring and desirable, a creature of her own fantasy with a fantasy lover all her own.

"I don't know," she wailed helplessly. Unfortunately, her fantasy was circumscribed by her own lack of experience.

Kneeling over her, Cole took her hand in his and carried it to his chest. She felt the diamond pattern of crisp dark hair that arrowed down to his waist and below. Slowly, he moved her palm over his small hard male nipples, then guided it lower, to where he wanted her attention.

She gave it freely, lovingly, testing his powers of resistance and her own powers to arouse—first with feathery fingertip caresses, then with the judicious use of fingernails. Finally—irresistibly—with a lingering series of kisses that brought him to a state near catatonia.

"God in heaven, woman, what are you trying to do, cripple me for life?"

"How'm I doing so far?" She teased him with a smile.

"You need to ask?"

He moved away abruptly, and she remembered the small, important packets on the bedside table. A moment later, he turned to her again. This time, instead of positioning himself over her, he settled back against the headboard and lifted her astride his thighs. "All right?" he murmured. His hands cupped her breasts while his tongue made love to her nipples.

Moments later they were both breathing harshly, quivering on the edge of the precipice. He cupped her hips and lifted her again, this time positioning her perfectly. It was like setting a torch to dry grass. Together they set a pace that could only be described as fast, frantic and furious. All too quickly, she felt herself flying over the top, heard the series of soft, wild cries that issued from her throat.

And then she collapsed against his chest, her head on his shoulder. Eventually they toppled together onto the bed. Cool air gradually chilled the perspiration on both their bodies, not that either of them noticed.

At some point before morning, one of them—later, neither could remember doing it—managed to pull up the covers.

The first thing Marty saw when a shaft of spring-scented sunshine found its way into the room was the two unused condoms on the bedside table. Cole was watching her, his expression a little cocky, a little wary. "Waste not, want not?" he suggested.

"Um…measure twice, cut once?" she returned.

"Ouch. I'm not sure I like the sound of that."

She grinned. "It's your saying."

"Yeah, well, I can't think of one that fits the circumstances, so how about if I make one up for the occasion?"

"Does it have anything to do with food? Because I missed out on dessert last night, and I'm hungry."

He nodded thoughtfully, his streaky-blond hair standing on end, dark bristles covering the lower half of his face. "Yeah, me, too. But first, tell me this—have you got any objection to being proposed to over bacon and eggs?"

Her heart stuttered, skipped a beat and began to pound. "That depends on what you're proposing," she said cautiously.

"Because I can do it just as well over waffles, even the frozen kind, if you'd rather."

She recognized the glint in his eyes now. "Does this have anything to do with your contract?"

He nodded. "Manner of speaking, I guess it does. See, what I'm after is an extension. Maybe fifty years or so, with an exclusivity clause."

She pretended to think about it while she fought against the absurd urge to cry. She'd had moonlight and roses. She'd had candlelight and French cuisine. None of those had lasted. She had a feeling this was the real deal—finally.

"Bacon and eggs sounds, um, reasonable," she ventured.

"Is that a yes or a no?"

They were still bare from the waist up, covered only by a yellow print sheet and a quilted spread from the waist down. "What are you waiting for? You want me to go first?"

Well, she did and she didn't. Talk of fifty-year contracts

was scary enough; she would prefer a bit of plain-speaking before she jumped to any conclusions. "I want to know if you've got the courage to say it in plain English."

"You mean the L word? As in lust?"

She had to laugh, because they both knew which L word she'd meant. And then he said it—the right L word—and her throat thickened up again with tears. Oh, God, she hated it when her emotions took over this way. What had happened to the pragmatic Virgo who always followed the rules and tried to stay out of trouble?

"Cole, you might as well know that I never rush into things. I'm far too practical for that."

He lifted one dark eyebrow. She rolled her eyes.

"Okay, maybe 'practical' isn't the right word, but I do know better than to act on impulse."

This time his other eyebrow lifted.

She gave up. "All right! But there's a lot about me you don't know. Such as I never—that is, I usually don't…rush into things. Honestly."

"Gotcha. We take it easy, get to know each other—you tell me all your bad habits, I gloss over mine." His smile was purely wicked.

She swatted him, and he laughed. "You want to hear it again?"

"Hear what again?"

"The L word?" he teased.

She shook her head, her heart too full for words. She knew the difference between loving and falling in love. One was permanent. The other was all too often an illusion.

She suffered from both.

But when she saw him reach across to the bedside table, she had to laugh, too.

"How hungry did you say you were?" he asked.

"Not all *that* hungry. Not for food, at least."

His eyes said it all. "That's my woman. My Marty. My love."

* * * * *

Harlequin on Location

hot tips

Wherever your dream date location, pick a setting and a time that won't be interrupted by your daily responsibilities. This is a special time together. Here are a few hopelessly romantic settings to inspire you—they might as well be ripped right out of a Harlequin romance novel!

Bad weather can be so good.

Take a walk together after a fresh snowfall or when it's just stopped raining. Pick a snowball (or a puddle) fight, and see how long it takes to get each other soaked to the bone. Then enjoy drying off in front of a fire, or perhaps surrounded by lots and lots of candles with yummy hot chocolate to warm things up.

Candlelight dinner for two...in the bedroom.

Romantic music and candles will instantly transform the place you sleep into a cozy little love nest, perfect for nibbling. Why not lay down a blanket and open a picnic basket at the foot of your bed? Or set a beautiful table with your finest dishes and glowing candles to set the mood. Either way, a little bubbly and lots of light finger foods will make this a meal to remember.

A Wild and Crazy Weeknight.

Do something unpredictable...on a weeknight straight from work. Go to an art opening, a farm-team baseball game, the local playhouse, a book signing by an author or a jazz club—anything but the humdrum blockbuster movie. There's something very romantic about being a little wild and crazy—or at least out of the ordinary—that will bring out the flirt in both of you. And you won't be able to resist thinking about each other in anticipation of your hot date...or telling everyone the day after.

Looking for a seductive cocktail?

hot tips

Try **Ero-Desiac**— a dazzling martini

With its warm apricot walls yet cool atmosphere, Verlaine is quickly becoming one of New York's hottest nightspots. Verlaine created a light, subtle yet seductive martini for Harlequin: the Ero-Desiac. Sake warms the heart and soul, while jasmine and passion fruit ignite the senses....

The Ero-Desiac

Combine vodka, sake, passion fruit puree and jasmine tea. Mix and shake. Strain into a martini glass, then rest pomegranate syrup on the edge of the martini glass and drizzle the syrup down the inside of the glass.

COMING NEXT MONTH

#1639 SOCIETY-PAGE SEDUCTION—Maureen Child
Dynasties: The Ashtons
When dashingly handsome billionaire Simon Pearce was deserted at the altar, wedding planner Megan Ashton filled in for the bride. Before long, their faux romance turned into scorching passion. Yet little did Simon know Megan had not only sparked excitement between his sheets, she'd also brought scandal to his door....

#1640 A MAN APART—Joan Hohl
The moment rancher Justin Grainger laid eyes on sexy Hannah Deturk, he vowed not to leave town without getting into her bed. Their whirlwind affair left them both wanting more. But Hannah feared falling for a loner like Justin could only mean heartache…unless she convinced him to be a man apart no longer.

#1641 HER *FIFTH* HUSBAND?—Dixie Browning
Divas Who Dish
She had a gift for picking the wrong men…her four failed marriages were a testament to her lousy judgment. So when interior designer Sasha Lasiter met stunningly sexy John Batchelor Smith she fervently fought their mutual attraction. But John was convinced Sasha's fifth time would be the charm— only if he was the groom!

#1642 TOTAL PACKAGE—Cait London
Heartbreakers
After being dumped by her longtime love, photographer Sidney Blakely met the total package in smart, and devastatingly handsome Danya Stepanov. Before long he had Sidney spoiled rotten, but she couldn't help wondering whether this red-hot relationship could survive her demanding career.

#1643 UNDER THE TYCOON'S PROTECTION—Anna DePalo
Her life was in danger, but the last person proud Allison Whittaker wanted to protect her was her old crush, bodyguard Connor Rafferty. Having been betrayed by Connor before, Allison still burned with anger, but close quarters rekindled the fiery desire that raged between them…and ignited deeper emotions that put her heart in double jeopardy.

#1644 HIGH-STAKES PASSION—Juliet Burns
Ever since his career-ending injury, ex-rodeo champion Mark Malone walked around with a chip on his shoulder. Housekeeper Aubrey Tyson arranged a high-stakes game of poker to lighten this sexy cowboy's mood— but depending on the luck of the draw, she could wind up in his bed…!

SDCNM0205